I0570858

WHO'S YOUR DADDY ANTHOLOGY

Each story is unique, witty and told with enough heat and emotional tone to keep readers engrossed in the pages. An insightful thought-provoking read and a wonderful book to add to your keeper file...
~ *Romance Junkies*

...three talented authors of erotica. Each adds a perfect addition to the anthology that centers on the very serious issue of infertility. This is a nice blend of romance and spice to please many fans across the romance genre... ~ *NovelTalk*

I would definitely recommend this book for a fast paced, fun and sexy read... ~ *Simply Romance Reviews*

Three of erotic romance's best authors come together in one volume. The stories are hot enough to leave you breathless. ~ *Author, Carol Lynne*

Total-E-Bound Publishing titles from these authors:

By Alexis Fleming

Sink or Swim
Sexy Mythconceptions: Hit and Miss
Sexy Mythconceptions: Pandemonium

By Lyn Cash

Sexy Mythconceptions: Hit and Miss
Sexy Mythconceptions: Pandemonium
Kinky Kruising: Mistress Mine
Kinky Kruising: The Big O

WHO'S YOUR DADDY

DIRECT DEPOSIT
SUMMER DEVON

STRATEGIC WITHDRAWAL
ALEXIS FLEMING

PLAYING THE ACE
LYN CASH

WHO'S YOUR DADDY ANTHOLOGY
ISBN # 978-1-906590-26-0
Direct Deposit ©Copyright Summer Devon 2008
Strategic Withdrawal ©Copyright Alexis Fleming 2008
Playing the Ace ©Copyright Lyn Cash 2008
Cover Art by Anne Cain ©Copyright 2008
Interior text design by Claire Siemaszkiewicz
Total-E-Bound Publishing

Published in 2008 by Total-E-Bound Publishing 1 Faldingworth Road, Spridlington, Market Rasen, Lincolnshire, LN8 2DE, UK.

DIRECT DEPOSIT

Summer Devon

Dedication

To Sunny and Lex. Thanks! Also to my three
fluffernutterpeanutbutter punkin pies who'll never read
this so I can call them whatever I want here.
So there, boys.

Also, to any reader who's still reading this dedication. If
you're facing infertility, don't actually haul off and
punch anyone who says "you know you just have to
relax." Contact these people instead:
http://www.resolve.org

Chapter One

"Fuck." That was the right word. "Fuck this." Zack relished the way the words filled his empty apartment. He stared at his laptop's screen and marvelled at how the simple arrangement of letters could create the sensation of a kick in the gut.

He shouldn't have been surprised to find Colleen Madison's name on the list of the fertility clinic's clients who were willing to be contacted for an interview. Well, well, so the Madisons had eventually gone to professional donors.

Good to see outside confirmation that his own donation to Colleen and Tyler's breeding efforts hadn't taken. Thank God for little blessings—or lack of them.

Zack clicked from the page to a blank screen. He'd email a pitch to everyone on the list except the Madisons, and he began typing a bland note requesting an interview. The feature assignment struck him as pure fluff, not his favourite sort of story, but he needed the money and this magazine paid well.

Dear Parent, he began, then sat back in his chair and stared at nothing—and saw the gorgeous Colleen.

When he'd met her, all three of them had been in college and she'd been Tyler's girlfriend. Zack had been taking British Literature that semester and had decided her quiet beauty belonged in another century.

She wasn't like other women. Even the way she'd pulled up her brown hair and attached it to the back of her head with a complex arrangement of pins was different, old fashioned. The pile of hair looked right with her pale skin, small rosebud mouth, and delicate features. Apparently he had some desire to bang a Victorian because back then he'd get hard just thinking about her graceful throat.

Ha. Maybe if he hadn't lusted after her for years the whole stupid incident wouldn't still bug him.

He hit backspace and tried again.

Hello, My name is Zack Reese and I am writing a piece about the offspring of sperm donor number sixty-nine. I hope I can talk to you about your child.

"Lame." Backspace, delete.

He returned to the email with the list of names. Her phone number was local. Funny, he'd thought they'd moved. Maybe he should just see what they'd say…No, he was not interested in calling.

He pushed back the chair and went into the kitchen. Rummaging around the fridge, he found a bottle of seltzer. He flipped the cap into the trash and gulped down half the bottle thinking about his one foray into a marriage bed. The best that could be said of the bizarre adventure was that it wasn't his marriage or his bed.

It had started without a hint of weirdness. Lonely in the new town, he'd run into Tyler at the gym. Tyler had never been Zack's favourite human—they had been on the college hockey team together — but he'd been glad to see a familiar face and they'd talked as they'd worked out.

After that, the three of them had gone out for dinner occasionally. Wolfing down pizza, Zack and Tyler had talked a lot about nothing in particular, sports, cars, sports cars, the usual entertaining but insignificant shit. Colleen had contributed the occasional quiet, dead-on remark.

At the gym, Tyler had soon become chummier. He'd creeped Zack out with all the questions about his sex life and health — until Zack had demanded to know why the hell Tyler wanted to know about his last AIDS test.

That's when the man had let it spill.

Colleen had wanted Zack. And Tyler hadn't minded his wife trying Zack out. No threesome action, Tyler had assured him. Just Zack and Colleen and they had his blessing to go bareback. As long as Zack showed him a clean bill of health.

He'd done it — he'd been stupid and horny enough to get a lab report from his goddamn doctor. Zack could still remember the moment he'd known it would happen. He'd been woman-free for weeks — his recent ex-girlfriend had gotten tired of his commitment phobia. At that instant he'd understood that even if he hadn't been the randiest thing on two feet, he'd have said yes to making Colleen. That was probably the moment he should have figured out he wanted her too much.

Hell. Even now, three years after the Colleen and Tyler fiasco, he felt stirrings when he thought of her. He grimaced down at his stiffening cock. Jesus, why would thinking about that sexual disaster half arouse him?

He finished the seltzer and decided to go for a run. Maybe he'd do some editing on a brochure when he got back. The story about donor sixty-nine's babies could wait until the next day. He didn't want to think about fertilisation at the moment.

He let himself out of the duplex and started a slow easy jog that should let him go at least ten miles. Slow burn was always better. But even after he hit the high school track, Colleen remained stuck in his head. The old anger and amusement came back full-force when he thought of that night.

It had started out strange and gotten stranger. At very least, the Madisons could have turned on soft music or fed him before they'd gotten what they'd wanted from him. Not that he'd needed any bribes. It was enough that Tyler had invited him over and had made it clear that Zack would get lucky. Zack would get to nail the woman of his dreams.

Yeah, that's just how he'd thought of it, too. Nailing her. He'd been Mr. Maturity back then. He'd had two beers to help him with his first big adventure as a Don Juan, screwing another man's wife with no latex to blunt the heat and sensation of Colleen.

Tyler had met him at the door and he'd given Zack a handshake that would have hurt like hell if he hadn't promptly squeezed back. That was Tyler's style — always competitive. Hyper-testosterone. They'd sat around in the tastefully decorated living room, drinking beer and making desultory conversation about hockey. After downing beer, he'd gathered the courage to ask, "Where's Colleen?"

"She's waiting for you, Sport. Go get her."

He'd slowly climbed the stairs. Tyler had followed right behind, and the skin on Zack's back crept but he hadn't said a word.

He should have been more alert to the extreme weirdness when he'd caught sight of her. She'd been dressed only in a

T-shirt and lay on her back on the bed, knees up, as rigid as a patient on a doctor's table.

But the sight of that slender, half-naked body and pale skin gleaming had intoxicated him more than the beers he'd downed that night.

"Hi, Zack." She aimed a tiny smile at him then reached over and turned off the light next to the bed. He'd been examining her, but when the only light came from the hall, he could barely make out her shape.

He wanted to protest but her next words stopped him. "Come on," she whispered. "It's fine this way."

He leaned over and whispered, "Really? What about Tyler?" It felt totally weird having the man there.

Tyler had heard him. "It's okay, guy," he said in a regular voice that boomed through the dark room.

Zack didn't want to appear uptight. He could be cool about this. Better than sneaking around behind the husband's back, Zack told himself. And the dark would hide the details.

He stripped naked, then, slipped onto the bed next to her, gathered her slender body in his arms and began hungrily kissing her mouth. She twisted her face away with a tiny protesting sigh.

"All right if I touch you?" he whispered.

"Yes. Please."

Okay, fine. He didn't think he was such a bad kisser, but hell, at least she let him caress her. Breathing hard, he pushed up the shirt, stroked her skin then ran his hand and his mouth down her body to feel what he couldn't see. He kissed her perfect tits, suckled her hardening nipples.

"You're so delicious," he whispered, resting his head between her breasts. "Thank you for tonight."

She made some kind of noise, maybe a groan and twitched up her hips. "Thank *you*," she muttered.

Fine. He kissed his way to her pussy. Her scent, the heat, alcohol in his blood and sheer speed of the whole scene went straight to his head. He kissed her gorgeous pussy, so fine and lovely. He circled her small clit with his thumb and breathed in her scent with reverence.

"No, you don't have to." Her voice came from far away and he just smiled and continued his work. Licking and sucking the tastiest treat he'd ever had.

"No, it's okay." She panted between words.

"Better than okay," he assured her. "Sweet, salty, sour, perfect."

"Please," she sounded choked now. "God. Please just do it."

He eagerly pushed himself up to kneel over her. "You sure you don't want me to wear a—"

"Go on, Zack." A man's impatient growl startled him. Tyler was still in the room, over by the wall. "Do it."

And he did. Probably couldn't have stopped himself even if Tyler had climbed onto his back. Thank God the jackass didn't.

It marked the first and only time Zack ever had sex without a condom. Hot, wet, unbelievable fucking. He settled between her legs. With some difficulty because she was so tight, he slid into her, achingly slow. Every sensitive inch of his skin touched the actual flesh inside a woman for the first time.

"God, you're perfect, Colleen," he whispered in her ear and he tried to reach down to touch her swollen clit. He wasn't going to last long pushing into her tight hot sweetness.

"You-you don't have to touch me there," she whimpered. "Please."

"Let him," Tyler said.

Zack knew he was part of the deal, but he wished he'd go the hell away. At least he wasn't there on the bed with them.

Tyler said, "You know it might help if you come, Coll."

Help? This confirmed what he'd suspected. Tyler was one peculiar fuck. Had he forced Colleen into taking on Zack?

She squeezed her eyes tight and then Zack, used to the dim light, saw the tear forming in the corner of her eyes. "What's wrong? Am I hurting you?" he whispered softly so Tyler wouldn't hear. "I should stop."

"No, it feels good. Oh, it-it's not supposed to..." She drew in a shuddering sigh.

He was on the edge of explosion already. His body screamed *move*, but he stilled, deep inside her, belly pressed to belly. "What?"

But then she twisted under him and dragged her heel over his calf. "Come on," she said, sounding almost furious. "Harder. Come in me hard. That's what we're doing, right?"

When she moved under him and talked about coming he just about lost it. And only a couple of thrusts later, he emptied deep inside her. Yeah, it was mortifying he hadn't lasted but far worse was she sobbed now. "Colleen,'" he pleaded. "I'm sorry. What's wrong?"

Someone touched his shoulder. "You done? Great, dude! My turn with her."

Colleen's arms lightly embraced Zack for a second. Her soft lips touched the corner of his mouth. "Thank you," she said. "You were nice to help us."

That word again. "Help you?"

Zack slipped from her when he felt the weight shift on the bed and noticed Tyler now naked from the waist down, perched next to them, frantically massaging his dick. Zack stood and backed away as Tyler push into Colleen who stared at the ceiling.

Zack watched Tyler start to fuck Colleen. He felt dizzy. He wanted out of the bedroom immediately, but he had to know. "Colleen. What do you mean help you?"

Tyler pumped hard now. He reached down and looped her leg over his shoulder. "Come on," he panted. "Come with me, honey. Don't lose it."

She didn't seem to pay attention to her husband thrusting into her. She shifted her head to the side and looked into Zack's eyes. Her porcelain forehead wrinkled. "Help us have a baby," she said.

"Shit." Zack gave an incredulous laugh. How else could he respond? "Of course. Christ. Oh. Shit. Why didn't you use a turkey baster?"

Colleen gasped. She wiggled under her husband. "What? What did—"

Tyler grunted, then answered Zack, thrusting into his wife with each word. "Direct. Works better. You had fun. Sports. For you. Zack."

Zack found his T-shirt on the floor and jammed it over his head. "Are you trying to inject your load in there too? That's why you're going for the sloppy seconds?"

"Didn't. You. Know?" Colleen's words were broken up by the impact of her husband ploughing hard into her.

"Hell no." He found the rest of his clothes and yanked them on, trying to ignore Tyler's pumping, naked butt. "But I get it now."

"Stop," she was saying, but Zack wasn't interested anymore. Colleen's anxious voice came in gasps while her husband thrust harder. "Ty, didn't you tell him? Wait, Zack, I'm sorry, what—Tyler, stop. Get out."

"Just. A moment. More. Uh." Tyler moaned, shuddered and went still. He hadn't lasted much longer than Zack, but lasting for pleasure hadn't been the point of the exercise.

Zack buckled his belt and wondered why he felt so used. Clear enough why he felt like an idiot.

Screw it, he'd figure out his own weird anger later. He felt nauseated in the room that smelled of sex and her perfume.

"Been extremely bizarre. Thanks, I suppose. Bye." Without looking back, he'd waved and taken off.

He hadn't returned any calls from the Madisons, though he had listened to the message about how he wasn't going to be a bio daddy. That was the word Tyler had used.

He had no interest in seeing either of them again. It was easy enough to avoid the gym Tyler haunted and Zack had managed to not run into them since.

After three miles of thumping around the track he realised he was still thinking about the Madisons. Colleen Madison. About her low, throaty laughter. About her on that bed. Enough. He didn't want this bullshit in his brain. He'd thought he'd left it behind—a misunderstanding, a fantasy about being a hot sex toy that turned into a farce—but he knew that night had changed him.

Maybe his over-inflated male ego had suffered a major deflation. She hadn't really desired him, only wanted his DNA. Or perhaps after that night with Colleen, he'd finally comprehended the whole baby-making aspect of fucking.

Whatever the reason, his enjoyment of the easy fun ended. No more casual sex for him. He looked at women as potential damned co-breeders, not just as fun playmates.

This became even more obvious to him a few months back when Phoebe, his last girlfriend, had gone off to New York City for a job. They'd talked about a long distance relationship—visiting each other when they could. Phoebe had made it clear she also wanted to have some fun with men she met in her new city.

The old Zack would have had no problem with that. He'd have said great, and he'd do the same. *Just use condoms, sweetie.* Now, he'd said, "no thank you and good luck." He missed the hell out of Phoebe, but even if she moved back here, he wouldn't start up a relationship with her again.

Not marriage material? Then no, thank you.

He was as bad as the most uptight woman he'd ever met, and that would probably be Colleen Madison — that one bizarre episode aside.

The Madisons owed him something, at least a "sorry we helped you make an ass of yourself that night."

He laughed aloud and veered off the path to head for home, skipping the last couple of miles of the run. Why not? He'd push the confrontation see if he could get them to apologise. At worst, he could only make a fool of himself again.

Dripping with sweat, he stopped on the way to the shower to compose a quick email, asking if they could meet. Less than an hour later, he logged on to work and discovered he already had his reply. She'd invited him over at noon. He rubbed his chin and wondered how many times Colleen Madison would make him feel like an idiot before he'd learn to stay away. Once more, at any rate.

Chapter Two

Colleen refused to worry. She cleaned the house then went out back to weed the garden. She'd taken the whole day off from the insurance company where she worked to get ready for an open house the next day. Now that local housing prices were heading up, she'd arranged to put the house on the market again and get out of the place she couldn't afford.

She was not going to worry about Zack's visit.

As she backhanded weeds into the compost heap, she thought about him. There was the time she'd watched Zack and Tyler play Frisbee. Nonsense, she hadn't watched Ty — her only recollection of that day had been of Golden Boy Zee flipping the disc as if he'd been born to play.

Not long before that Frisbee match, Tyler had suggested to her that their old college pal, 'the golden boy' their private nickname for him, might work as a donor. He'd said something about Zack having good genes even though the guy wasn't much of a thinker. She'd watched the golden boy idly at first then had begun to admire him. And then had found herself imagining carrying and raising the child of a man who smiled easily and honestly. "Shallow," Tyler had once called him, but it had occurred to her the word that fit was 'happy'.

As Zack had laughed and reached high for the Frisbee, his shirt had pulled from his jeans and she'd studied his muscular side, the sliver of his tanned flesh. The vivid image remained lodged in her memory and still made her body clench as if she'd been spinning in circles.

Back then, she'd felt sudden alarm at her response to the sight. She'd turned away from the Frisbee game and walked back to the car. Only much later, she'd understood she'd been fighting attraction.

Even when she'd understood her feeling, she'd tried to ignore it. It should have been easy to dismiss. Not only had she been married, but Zack had no interest in commitment and she hadn't understood how anyone could screw casually. To her it was all about relationships and love and flowers.

Flowers. Ha. She spotted one more dandelion and dug down deep to yank out the long taproot.

Now, years later, she had no interest in a serious relationship yet her body yearned for something. She probably wanted a man. If only she could arrange a meeting of bodies, and not minds...or rather, not emotions.

She flung the last weed hard into the pile. That's what she'd felt like for too long: a weed past its prime and fit only for compost. Not anymore. Self-pity and self-loathing had gotten too boring for words and she'd moved on.

Colleen liked the new, simple life she'd created. Yet lately her long-sought-after peace felt dull, so she'd gone to bars with friends who'd suggested sizzling, no-strings sex might rouse her nearly comatose libido. No luck. During her three expeditions to find potential bed-partners she'd only gotten headaches from loud music and drink.

The garden looked tidy enough so she went inside and showered. After trying on a pastel summer dress, then a slinky black number, she dressed in faded jeans and a red T-shirt. Nothing remotely sensual.

But why not let herself play sexy? The long-forgotten twinges of lust might be worth exploring. After all, she'd admired Zack's well-built body and his easy-going personality.

These days admiration didn't have to equal love, commitment…and family. She hoped it might equal hot, sweaty sex. Period.

As she combed her hair she imagined Zack's kisses and his hands on her breasts. His mouth, warm and eager, kissing them. She absently ran a hand over her nipple and it hardened under her palm. For the first time in ages, the thought of screwing made her body grow luxuriously heavy with desire.

She tossed the comb into the bathroom cupboard and headed downstairs to make more coffee. There was no way she'd slink up to that particular man and press herself against him — Colleen would never again use Zack as anything more than fantasy material.

When he appeared at her door, she would not act awkward. Nor would she jump him. She paused on the stairs and grinned as she imagined backing him against a wall and climbing his body. And then he'd swat her to the floor.

Who'd blame him?

She looked at her watch, a thick Timex Tyler had left behind. Maybe Zack wasn't even going to show up — a relief and disappointment. But then, five minutes later, he was there.

Colleen drew three full breaths before she could bring herself to answer his knock. How would he act?

She bet he hadn't forgotten the stupid night she and Tyler had managed to make idiots of themselves. But she wondered if Zack also remembered the time when he'd gotten absolutely stinko. He'd banged on her door at 10 p.m. and begged to stay in her room. She'd been worried about him and had convinced Tyler they should stay with Zack instead of going to spend the night in Tyler's room.

They'd been friends, sort of. Back then.

She opened the door and smiled, so nervous her mouth was dry.

"Hey," he said and looked down at her with absolutely no expression on his face.

Surely he'd gotten taller. Or perhaps he'd only filled out across the shoulders, grown more solid. Even skinny, he'd been all fluid grace. Now he was intimidating and probably just as comfortable with his body. A potent mix.

She stepped back to let him in, wishing she could think of the right greeting.

"Thank you for getting in touch," she managed at last. "I'm so glad you did." Not necessarily true. But then he returned her smile, revealing his impossibly white teeth. There. He hadn't actually snarled when he saw her, so maybe it wasn't a mistake to invite him over.

She walked towards the kitchen, too nervous to turn around to see if he followed.

From close behind her he said, "You cut your hair." He sounded almost disappointed. Had he liked it long?

She automatically ran fingers through her shoulder-length, wavy hair. "Yes. This is a lot easier to deal with." At the door to the kitchen she stopped and he almost ran into her. She turned and...Wow. His eyes, cool and blue, met hers. Heat from his body, the aura of menace or maybe just sex, slammed into her. Alarm systems went off inside her. *Warning! Dive! Hide!* She practically scampered across the small kitchen to escape.

"Coffee?" she asked, praying he'd say yes. What else could she give him? Water or dust, maybe. And if they just sat and looked at each other, she'd give into a fit of the screaming meemies.

"Sure," he said standing in the middle of the floor. She had to scoot around his body to get to the cups. He didn't seem to mind or even notice. He just stood, hands shoved into the back pockets of his worn jeans looking around the room.

He'd been so eager the night he'd screwed her, almost as if he'd had a crush on her. Hard to imagine now. Colleen felt a twinge of irritation. If he was so bored or disgusted by her why'd he show up at all? She considered asking him, but she wanted to get rid of that unpleasant bit of past business first. Her apology.

After solemnly pouring two cups of coffee, though God knew she wanted something stronger, she began her rehearsed talk.

"Zack. Uh. It was a while ago. The last time we met and you might not remember how strange it was, but I wanted to say I am sorry about the time that you and I ah—"

"Might not remember how strange it was? What the hell?" He gave a bark of laughter. "How could I forget?"

She fumbled as she picked up the cups and some hot coffee splashed onto her fingers. "Well, I don't know. You could have—maybe you had a lot of encounters back then. Tyler mentioned you'd been drinking beer that night. I mean I know you were careful and didn't do thousands of—" This did not sound good. She was trying to apologise, not accuse him of being a horn dog. He *was*, of course, but that wasn't the point. "Anyway, I always felt like Tyler and I owed you an apology."

He muttered something under his breath, maybe "that was easy," but she couldn't be sure.

She handed him his coffee, and pointed at the breakfast bar. "Want to sit?"

He nodded. They crossed the kitchen and perched on the tall stools at the breakfast bar — or rather she perched, feeling ridiculous. His long legs meant he could just lean his butt against the seat. No one had ever managed to look comfortable on the stupid stools before. Figured he'd be the first.

He still looked around the nearly empty room avidly, as if trying to find evidence of her existence. Good luck to him. She'd erased all traces of the past life — always best when putting a house up for sale or finally recovering from the bad end of a marriage.

Zack cleared his throat and drummed his fingers on the granite countertop. He rolled his head from side to side, almost as if he wanted to draw her attention to the strong column of his neck.

She couldn't look away even if she wanted to. How strange that he was twitchy too. He'd always seemed so comfortable in his own skin and *he* had no reason to be nervous now.

At last he broke the uncomfortable silence. "About that night. The thing that bothers me most. I thought it was for just, um, fun. So how come you two didn't tell me what you really wanted?"

Direct. She'd forgotten how he didn't mess around and went straight to the heart of a matter. Not a subtle guy, Tyler had said about him.

She was grateful to Zack for not just smiling politely and changing the subject, but she didn't want to talk about how ugly things had gotten. So she picked her words carefully. "After you left that night, Tyler told me what he'd done. I thought you knew what was going on, why we asked you to help, but it turned out he hadn't wanted to talk about the infertility with you. After he admitted he hadn't told you our plans, it became clear he was embarrassed. A lot of things embarrassed him, I think. As if we should be ashamed because we couldn't get pregnant."

She snorted. "I don't know what made him think he could hide what he'd planned that night from both of us. All I can say is he hated talking about a lot of what was going on, even with me."

She picked up her cup and drank to keep herself from saying more. The last thing she wanted was to sound like a bitter ex-wife. She'd had enough of that role.

Maybe Tyler had been right and tip-toeing around uncomfortable subjects wasn't a bad idea. She smiled brightly and said, "Well, so. In the email you sent this morning you mentioned getting my name from the clinic. How's the article going?"

"Fine."

"I noticed your by-line in the paper a year or so ago. I was surprised to learn you decided to become a writer. I'd always thought you'd planned to become a P.E. teacher or something."

He shrugged. "I'm free-lance now. I like working on my own." He absently stirred his coffee and continued to look around the kitchen. "How's your kid?"

Instead of sipping, she gulped the coffee and burned her tongue. "What? What makes you think I've got a child?"

"The article I'm writing is about sperm donor sixty-nine's numerous offspring. You've got one of them, right?"'

"Who told you that?" Oh, no. She didn't mean to sound so tense. This was old pain, after all. No longer raw.

He frowned then seemed to notice her tension and gave her an apologetic smile. "The clinic. They gave me your email as someone to contact about sixty-nine's successful donations." His voice softened. "I'm sorry if they put you on the wrong list. That's pretty rotten."

"Yes, they were wrong. No baby." She waited for the familiar spasm of sorrow to pass, a tiny echo of stronger, past grief. "We did try with that donor's sperm for one cycle, but then…"

"What?" He'd stopped fidgeting and it was as if he actually focused on her for the first time since walking in the front door.

She stalled again by sipping her coffee. Was it any of his business? Maybe the question she should ask was what the heck could he or anyone else do with the information. Nothing, she supposed. It wasn't a success story for his article about the donor.

She put down the cup and met his blue eyes, seeing flecks of green she'd never noticed before. Then again, she'd purposefully not made a practice of studying Zack's eyes. She allowed her gaze to shift so she could think more clearly. "Tyler and I broke up a long time ago. I mean it had been coming for a long time. The worst was the night you came over. Oh." She turned bright red. So much for thinking clearly. "Jeepers, that sure sounded wrong."

But it must have been the right thing to say because it broke some sort of tension for him. His laughter sounded real now. "Yeah, I got the impression you'd have rather been anywhere else but under me."

She didn't know she could feel any more embarrassed. Though actually hearing him speak the phrase 'under me' brought on a ripple of something more interesting, a heavy thickening in her lower belly she hadn't felt for so long.

She had to explain. "It wasn't that I hated it with you. It was the whole thing. It wasn't you. I meant…I remember you felt—" Whoops. Could she do a more terrible job of this?

She grabbed at the coffee mug and lifted it to her mouth to stop herself from saying any more stupid words. But as she drank the last of it, she examined him hopefully.

"Okay," he said, casual as can be, the small hint of a smile on his mouth. "I'm listening."

He was a player, right? So that incident couldn't have hurt him deeply. And here he was in her kitchen, drinking her coffee, smiling at her.

Unbidden, the thought of being allowed to touch him and of him touching her, drifted into her mind. She might pull him into a hug and feel his broad shoulders, his muscular arms around her.

Whoa, just the flash of that image and her body went into unaccustomed high gear—the backs of her knees weakened, her pussy swelled. Maybe someday soon she'd even make an attempt to get him into her bed again. After all, he didn't seem to hate her.

In the meantime, she owed him the truth. This time she'd be direct, like him. No hiding or half-lies.

Sucking in a deep breath, she began. "I haven't told anyone else all the details. But I guess…if you're interested."

"I am," he said.

"The trouble began months before that night with you. Tyler and I had been trying to get pregnant for years. We wanted kids early, right after we got married, which was right after we finished college."

"I remember," he said, still smiling, and she felt herself turn red. He hadn't been invited to the wedding.

27

"Anyway, we stopped using birth control the night of our honeymoon." She rubbed at a chip in the pale mauve nail polish on her thumb. "It was fun at first, really." She caught sight of his scowl and went quickly on. "Yeah, I know. Too much information. But you did want to know why it happened...why I behaved so oddly that night, right?"

"Sure." His casual tone was contradicted by his intense and disconcerting attention focused on her. Her body prickled with long forgotten awareness.

He nudged her back to the conversation. "Go on, then. Give me the whole history. I'm curious."

"For a year after we got married, it was great. But then it started to go south."

"What? The sex?"

"That. Everything." She fought the urge to change the subject—his steady gaze seemed to challenge her. Or maybe she'd forgotten what it was like to have a man pay such close attention to her words.

She pushed some loose strands of hair back behind her ear. "It became all about making a baby. Tyler wouldn't want to do anything with me on days when it didn't matter and I got tired of taking my temperature. We had all these tests done. His tests were no big deal, you know, he just had to, um, put some stuff into a cup."

A swift grin crossed his face—probably because she couldn't bring herself to say jack off or even ejaculate. He'd always been amused by what he'd called her prim and proper side.

She gave him a small smile in silent acknowledgement before continuing. "My tests were more invasive. I had two laparoscopies and biopsies and...well, medical procedures. You know about that stuff, I suppose, for that article you're writing." God, just using the language of infertility brought back that dreary time.

He nodded.

She continued, hoping she sounded laid-back about the whole thing—and was surprised to discover she succeeded. "They couldn't find anything wrong with us except his sperm count was slightly off. That's when he thought of getting a donor. I was tired of all the tests and the up and down cycle by then. Hope and misery. I wanted to take a break from it, or even think about adoption. I still think about that sometimes."

She stood and went to pour herself more coffee, though the way her heart raced, she definitely didn't need the caffeine. But she wanted to think, figure out how much more to tell him.

He shook his head and put a hand over his cup when she held up the carafe questioningly. "Go on," he said.

She walked back to the counter and climbed onto the stool. "Ty came up with the idea of using someone we knew. Save money and all that. And I think—no I'm sure, he thought it would be interesting. In the bedroom. You know, pep things up. Make it better, more exciting." She blushed. "He really didn't say anything about having all three of us in bedroom—but by then, we were pretty pathetic in bed and even worse at talking. He just said he thought you'd be a good donor and he told me he'd made sure you were clean."

She remembered that detail and frowned at him. "When I heard that, I figured you knew. I mean asking for a medical report was kind of clinical, right?"

"Oh." His grin broadened, but he didn't explain himself. He leaned back and folded his arms, his broad fingers spread at the inside of his elbows. Those hands that held her and touched her. She realised she held her breath as she watched him.

Fine. He didn't have to give an explanation for his behaviour that night, but she wanted to finish her confession. "The thing is, I told Tyler I didn't want to go to bed with you, certainly not for fun, because I wanted to work it out with us, with him and bringing in another man for pleasure didn't seem to be the way to do that. I agreed you would be a great donor but just a donor. He said I was uptight and that was part of our problem. Maybe he was right. I only knew I didn't want the rest of the experience. I didn't want to feel excitement with anyone other than him."

Oh great. She was so certain she had gotten over this nonsense and now her throat grew tight around a lump of emotion. "When you're infertile, a lot of people tell you to just relax. 'It'll happen if you just relax and have fun.' He used to say that, too. 'Lighten up. Make it a party' — even though we both were wound so tight. I once made him come when he wasn't inside my body." Her face grew red with embarrassment. "He was furious."

She examined the surface of her immaculate expensive counter and successfully squelched the old sorrow. "I think Ty wanted you to do it with me for a lot of reasons. I-I think it turned him on that someone else wanted his wife when the whole sex thing had become a chore. For us both. He convinced me to let you do it, um, the regular way. I thought it would be okay, but it wasn't." She risked a glance into his face. "When you touched me. Seemed to really enjoy touching me. I felt it."

His twisted smile now struck her as bitter, but he still didn't say anything.

She looked quickly down at her thumb and its chipped polish before his less-than-pleasant smile sapped the last of her courage.

"See, it wasn't right that it was you. It reminded me of what it's supposed to be. Being in bed. I-I wanted that with my *husband*, not with some pal. Sex to me is — was — nothing more than getting a deposit of fluid in the right spot. In out, in out, pump, pump, release. An exercise. Anything else — touching, kissing — had grown almost meaningless. Anyway, I didn't know you that well, but it felt like it meant something important when you stroked me. Meant too much. It felt too good."

Colleen edged back up onto the stool, only slightly mortified by her admission. She'd said enough — way more than enough. Let him speak.

"I think I understand," he said, every trace of belligerence gone from his voice. "Thank you for explaining."

He put down his cup and stood. Shit. Her heart sank. He'd gotten what he'd come for — probably reassurance that she *had* wanted him that night — and now he could leave.

She wasn't sure why she wanted him to stay. After all, she had promised herself not to make a fool of herself — yet she still tried to stop him. "Do you want something to eat? I don't have much. But there's bound to be something."

She slid off the stool and went to the fridge. Wow, a single lemon yoghurt, a quart of orange juice, a dried out slab of Jarlsberg cheese. Even more pathetic than usual.

From behind her he spoke. "Did you get it back?"

She shut the door and turned around. "Huh?"

"Did you and Tyler want each other again?"

"Didn't you hear me? We're divorced. We broke up two years ago."

"Okay. Tell me about the break up." He leaned a hip against the edge of the sink. "I got time."

Was there any '*I got to hear this*' hostility in the way his mouth pressed tight and his eyes narrowed?

"Uh. Can I get you—"

"No. I don't need food, I don't need drink." He smiled, and there was no bitterness in his face. On the contrary, she saw a glimmer of affection or something more stirring as he said, "And I'll understand if you don't want to talk."

"It's okay." She spread her hands over the counter, pressed her palms to the cool stone. Amazing this wasn't so hard to talk—now that she'd gotten started. "Not much more to say. Infertility took over everything. I wanted to move on, stop with the procedures and tests, he wanted to try more. I said I'd do IUI. Intrauterine insemination. Donor sperm mixed with his. Me taking Clomid, then spread out and tilted up on the table for an hour for two or three days a month, a tube going up into me. Not as dramatic as IVF but still a nuisance."

She heaved a sigh. "They found something might be wrong with me and suggested I have another laparoscopy before trying IUI again. But I was ready to stop. And then one day I did."

She felt her shoulders relax as she recalled that day when she knew she was ready to get off the roller coaster. "I was lying on my back on the doctor's table and just knew I was done. I told Ty, but he didn't believe me."

Zack moved closer to her, until he was less than three feet away from her in the large room. She watched his chest rise and fall with each breath, hardly caring that she stared. "That was the end?" he asked.

She raised her eyes to his. "We tried marriage counselling, but we weren't a team any more. No sex for anything other than making a baby, no common goals, I wasn't sure I really trusted him after that night with you...and other things. So that's that. The end of my marriage in a nutshell."

"And now?"

She gave a tiny shrug. The tension between them almost sucked the air from the room. Now, it was different. Zack knew everything, except how much she craved him. She didn't want to say the words, but perhaps he could sense her need. Heck the way her nipples announced her arousal, she might as well wear a neon sign. *Desperate Woman Here.*

Come on Zack, she thought. She didn't want to be the aggressor. It went against her nature — and anyway because of their past she knew any move had to come from him. So she looked at him with what she hoped was a sultry smile and wished he could read minds.

Please Zack. I want to fuck you. Let's get naked. Teach me about having fun. I lost that, and you can teach me.

Chapter Three

Zack looked at her sad, sweet smile. He didn't want to interview her for the goddamn story—he'd known that even before he'd shown up at her door. He wasn't sure what he wanted from her—well, yes, he knew exactly what he wanted, but his days of mindless screwing were over, he reminded himself. And he didn't want to play weird-ass emotional games no matter how attractive the prize was.

Time to say thanks for the coffee, the explanation and goodbye. But he didn't take off. Not yet. Stalling for time, Zack carried his cup to the sink. "Funny, I would never have guessed you would be the one to break up."

"It was a mutual decision."

"Yeah? So where did Tyler end up?"

"He moved to the Midwest. Indiana. He's married again and he recently wrote to say she's pregnant."

He didn't bother to hold back his snort of disgust. Her shoulders hunched again and he hastened to say, "The man's a twit."

For the first time since he'd gotten there, she laughed. "It's okay. We both were twits, and now I'm much better. I don't think Tyler and I brought out the best in each other."

"Nothing wrong with you."

"I can be reserved, I guess. I was sheltered when I was growing up. College was a wild new world for me. He was my first boyfriend, you know."

That explained a lot. "No, I didn't know."

"I liked how he could talk to anyone. And you can do that too. All those girls you went out with in college. You had fun. I didn't know how."

"You want me to teach you how to flirt?" He wondered when he'd lost his mind to be talking to Colleen Madison like this — flirting for fuck's sake.

Her brow furrowed. "I'm happy," she said slowly. "I don't think I need to change."

He couldn't help laughing at her serious response. "You sound like I offered to brainwash you. I wasn't going to try to train you to be some kind of trick pony."

She gave a tiny grimace. "I sounded sort of defensive, huh?"

"A tad."

"Well, okay, maybe I could use a few changes after all."

He didn't say anything. Her blue eyes, the turned down corners of her mouth, seemed weary. But the rest of her body looked just fine.

Maybe she didn't like the way he looked her up and down, because she shut her eyes and even turned her head to the side.

And then she shocked the hell out of him. "That night you touched me. Tried to kiss me. I think about it now, all the time. Still. Mostly I wish I'd let you actually kiss me. By then I'd already lost all interest in sex. I mean making love became a chore and a reminder of that horrible roller coaster. All of the hope and disappointment was too much after a while."

She licked her lips, a quick nervous motion with the tip of her tongue, unconsciously and outrageously erotic. "That night. You tried to wake up my body again, it was so intense. I couldn't. But when I think about it, about you…"

Her voice trailed off and her face went pink. When did she think about his touch? Perhaps in bed?

He smiled imagining the possibilities. Mm, very nice. "You were saying? What happens when you think about me?"

She opened her eyes and crossed her arms over her breasts. "When I do think about sex, I think about that night and how you adored my body. That's what it felt like — I was special."

"Felt that way to me." Damned if the sight of her still made him hard. That must be why he opened his mouth to admit the truth. "You were special. That's why that night was such a kick in the groin."

"I'm sorry. It was because we took advantage of you."

"No, that's not it. Not entirely anyway. You loathed having me touch you."

"Did I sound like I loathed it?"

He shrugged and tried to remember. "You just wanted my, uh, deposit."

She narrowed her eyes. "I told you. I still think about you. About what you did with your mouth."

Yes. Those words felt better than scoring a goal. Inside he pumped a fist in the air and gave a bloodcurdling yell of triumph. But he wasn't going to let her off easy. "I can't remember. What did I do with my mouth?"

She sounded angry when she answered. "You kissed me. Down there as if you liked it."

"Oh, I did like it a lot." He didn't bother to stop the leer that spread across his face and he took a step towards her.

She inched away from him—but not far. "Cunnilingus, Colleen. I like it. Good tasty oral sex. Yum."

He wondered why he was torturing the poor woman Not revenge—no, he did it because he enjoyed watching the goose bumps rise on the smooth skin of her arms. The quickening of her breath. She tried to hide her arousal and that made it even more...arousing.

"You're so much bigger than I remember. Taller," she murmured.

"Do I frighten you?" He gave her his best wicked, hungry wolf grin.

"A little."

He shoved his hands into his back pockets in a "nothing dangerous here" gesture, but he didn't back off. He liked being close enough to hear the uneven stutter of her breath and to feel and smell her fragrant warmth. "Hey now. You don't have to be scared of me. Didn't I tell you? I hated touching you when I thought you were reluctant."

"Mmm. But that's not what frightens me. I think just the idea of sex is sort of scary at this point. Intimidating."

"How long has it been since you had any?"

Colleen tilted her chin up as if showing him she had nothing to be ashamed of. "Since Tyler and I broke up. Three years."

Zack's smile vanished. "Aw, jeez, I'm sorry it's been so hard for you."

At his words, the strange tension between them broke or at least eased.

Was that a good thing or bad?

Colleen went to the sink and began to mess aimlessly with dishes. She put soap on the sponge and washed the coffeepot, began to wipe down the counter. "People do survive without sex, you know. I've been fine."

He moved close to her again. "Sure."

Colleen wasn't sure if he was agreeing with her or mocking her, but she gave a knee-jerk response. "Not all of us want to have meaningless sex."

He made a choking sound that sounded suspiciously like laughter.

She twisted around to face him. "Okay, never mind that last sanctimonious remark." With a roll of the eyes, she said, "I didn't mean to sound so holier than thou but I'm defensive, I guess. Or it's part of my upbringing. Truth is, I actually wouldn't mind something utterly meaningless." Her try at a sophisticated laugh came out like a nervous giggle.

He was so near her shoulder almost made contact with his arm. She drew in a deep breath and smelled soap and pure head-spinning Zack. He brushed a finger deliberately along her cheek. "But hey, Colleen, didn't you very recently say it didn't feel meaningless when I touched you?"

Her body's clamour started up again and made it difficult to think. "It felt—no, it doesn't matter about how it felt because we didn't know each other. It wasn't loving because we didn't..." Hold on. Hadn't she actually longed for this outcome? For a chance to feel Zack's body?

She fell silent and tried to steady herself so he wouldn't see how completely aroused she was just by being in the room with him.

She turned back to rinse the sponge under a stream of hot water.

"Colleen?"

She glanced into his serene face and resisted the urge to throw herself at him and admit the truth. *I am not okay anymore. God, I am so hungry, Zack.* Would she manage to ruffle him? Or perhaps his eyes would grow heavy-lidded and darken with desire.

She gave up the pretence of cleaning and tossed the sponge into the sink. The moment to make a move had come much earlier than she'd expected and she was going to grab it and maybe get a chance to grab him. "Um. I don't mind that casual attitude anymore. You know what friends with privileges means, Zack?"

"Sure. What century do you think I live in?"

"I didn't know what it meant until about a month ago. I'm still out of touch, I guess." She rushed on before she lost her nerve. "Anyway, friends with privileges. Would you like that? With no agenda. Just because we want to. A lot. Touch each other, I mean."

She'd thought she was ready for any response, but was still taken aback when he began to laugh again.

"You do laugh a lot," she said not sure if she should be insulted or join him. "Is this a with me or at me laugh?"

"It's funny," he insisted. "For God's sake, you sound like me a while back. Say, about three years ago."

"It's just that, well, it took a long time. But the thing is, I like my life." She licked her dry, tingling lips. "Alone. Independent. I don't want to change anything major."

"So you're suggesting we just do it for fun? Go to bed together." He spoke as if this were a novel concept. "Nothing interrupted, nothing destroyed by the sex. Hell. It's not like we're best friends. Not like we've talked any time in the last three years."

She couldn't drag her attention from his hands resting easily on his hips now. Those strong fingers would caress her again, at last. She hoped. But she had to ask, "Have I offended you? The way you said that. It sounded as if you don't even like me."

"I want you. I've always wanted you—even after that bizarre night I did. I've gotten sick of thinking about you, if you want the honest truth."

Her face grew hot, but she tried to stay casual. The gorgeous Zack had lusted after *her* for more than a few hours? What a concept. "And well? This might be a way to, ah, get me out of your system."

He shrugged, a loose-limbed easy motion that was oddly graceful. She owed him and more than that she wanted him—so much it made her belly twist and her heart beat too fast. Hunger and fear.

He'd read her thoughts and now she'd get her wish. But first she wanted to make this clear for them both. "Maybe what you're saying is we both want the same thing. We'd be—what's that phrase? We'd be fuck buddies?"

He loomed over her now. "Funny to hear you say fuck," he said softly. "You always seemed so lady-like."

"I'm not," she managed to say. "I don't want to be."

His large hands rested on her shoulders then gently, expertly, massaged her tight muscles, a light touch that sent thick heat plummeting straight to her pussy. Her useless womb grew heavy with eagerness. Ah, but this had nothing to do with tests and drugs and failure. Pure lust threatened to take control of her and she wanted to go crazy with it. She needed to taste him, feel him plunge into the slick mindless heat with her immediately.

Her fingers trembled as she reached up to slide her hand to the back of his neck. Nerves had turned her hands cold and his skin was gloriously hot and firm to the touch.

"Kiss me like you mean it," she whispered.

"Oh, I do." His breath touched her lips almost as gentle as the soft brush of his mouth a moment later. Warm soft lips pressed to hers.

She whimpered and the involuntary sound of her desire set off a response in them both. The gentle nibbling touch became a deep hungry kiss. His hands traced down her sides, over to her bottom, kneading, drawing her close, pulling her against him. Teasing turned into ravenous messy kisses — tasting of escalating hunger.

Her head spun and her skin demanded his touch. She had not lost control for such a long time. Never like this.

Panic sliced through her. Oh, God, she could barely breathe as she groped a man with an exotic, unfamiliar feel and scent. She didn't really know him, hadn't seen him in years and her cunt was swollen and wet for him. "Wait. Stop."

He released her at once and he even took a step away from her, panting.

"Right. Good idea. It's okay, Colleen. You want to do something else? Like um…" He rubbed the side of his face. "Go out for a walk or something? Or maybe I should just get going." Still breathing hard, he looked down at his watch.

She hugged herself. "No, please stay. I-I was just kind of frightened and I don't even know why. I'll be okay."

"You don't know why?"

She bit her lip. "Ever go on one of those rides where you get in and the seat thing comes down over you and just as it starts to speed up, you wonder if you've lost your mind?"

"There's nothing blocking you from escape, silly woman. You just say the word and I back off." He took another step back. "See?"

She nodded. "I trust you." Not entirely, but he didn't need to know that. "And actually it's not you I'm worried about. I'm the one who's losing it. I mean blasting off. Zoom." That was definitely not a lie. She managed a tentative grin, which drew one of his glorious smiles.

41

"That sounds very promising, blasting off. The sky's the limit." How'd he manage to get closer without her noticing?

His fingers brushed her forearm lightly. The tiny contact poured the heat back into her.

She swallowed hard. "Okay. I want to do this."

"Aw shit, I really do want you," he said, sounding angry.

"Yes, please, I want to. I'm not scared now." She was slightly, but to hell with fear. Never in her life had she been the aggressor but she had to feel him—and she had to convince him she had no plans to stop.

She laced her fingers in his and tugged him to the couch. He sat and she climbed on his lap, straddling him. He groaned. His hands traced her hips and again pulled her against him. They pressed close and kissed open-mouthed and hungry. But she wanted more of him.

With a wiggle, she escaped his embrace and crouched over him, unbuttoning his shirt with unsteady fingers, stopping to slide her hands over his skin. She felt a trace of soft hair on his chest and belly.

"I need you," she said to his skin. She whipped off her own shirt and scrambled out of her bra.

"Shit," he said again and his hands were on her breasts, thumbs circling her tightening nipples.

"Such romantic language," she murmured, leaning into him.

She could feel his smile against her neck. She wove her fingers into his hair. "Please," she whispered. "Kiss me."

"You turn me into an idiot, Colleen. Always have." At least he didn't sound resentful as he lowered his mouth to her breast.

She groaned. Their jeans rasped as she circled herself against his erection, the cloth almost grew hot. She reached between them to feel the solid heat of his bulge. When she touched the zipper, his mouth left her breast. The chill air hit her wet nipple and she hesitated. He gently reached for her hand and tucked his fingers around hers.

He looked up at her, his eyes dilated, his mouth curved into a smile. "Here's the deal. I'm not gonna fuck you."

"What?"

"Oh, I'll do all sorts of things with you, girl. But the fucking's fucked you up. I can't help thinking of you with your knees up like you were on some kind of doctor's—"

"I didn't want to enjoy it then. Now I do. A lot."

She scooted back onto his thighs, grabbed for his belt and missed.

He grabbed her wrists and didn't miss. "I have a plan, sort of. We're going to make out like rabid teens. We're going to neck."

"Mmm, oh, Zack. That sounds wonderful."

"And then we're going to go for a walk. And talk. And maybe hold hands."

She pulled her hands away from him. "But that's...that's." She wasn't sure what it was.

"It's called dating. Ever done it?"

"I don't know if I can do that." She got up from his lap and sat down heavily next to him. Her pussy thrummed with disappointed eagerness. "I feel all. Well. Dried up and I don't think I want that romantic stuff. I don't want to think."

"Okay, then I'll do the work."

"But I don't want a—" She stopped in time. No reason to offend him by saying she only wanted him for his body.

Turned out he could finish the sentence for her. "You don't want a relationship with me."

She bit her lip. "Not with anyone. It's not you. I'm just not ready to be with a man. Well, except in bed."

"Whoa, you're really something." He laughed. "You're a basket case, Colleen."

Her angry reply was almost out of her mouth, but she swallowed it. He had the right to a nasty come-back after she'd just insulted him. Besides, the way his words hurt, he could be right. She shrugged. "Yeah, maybe I am."

He stood. For a moment, she thought he'd walk out. She closed her eyes to stop the pain of watching him go. It shouldn't hurt so much. After all, it wasn't like watching her husband, the man she'd built her life around, walk out. But when she opened her eyes again, he hadn't moved. He continued to watch her. "Colleen," he said, serious and quiet. "You still think you want to screw me?"

"God. More than anything." The impulsive words came out before she could stop and think. She got to her feet so he couldn't tower over her like that.

"If you do, good. But I've decided. We're going to do it the way I want this time."

"Oh. But—"

He leaned close to her and whispered. "Don't get me wrong. I will make you come. I will make you scream with pleasure. But I am not going to fuck you. Not yet."

Chapter Four

Colleen whimpered and wondered if a person could pass out with lust. She pushed her fingers into Zack's hair trying to distract him and pull him into a kiss. She'd wondered about the texture of his hair, had longed to touch it and she wasn't surprised it felt smooth and silkier than her own. After a long wonderful kiss, he pulled away and even took a step back.

She folded her arms over her breasts. "Is this some kind of revenge?"

He grinned as if proud that she'd finally gotten the idea. "Heck, yeah. But it's more than that. Colleen. I don't want either one of us hurt, okay? Can you trust me?"

"I don't know."

"Hey, I'm willing to trust you. Don't you be a chicken."

She sighed and picked up her T-shirt.

As she pulled it over her head, he clucked at her.

"Okay, yes, I'm chicken," she said as she firmly tugged the bottom of the shirt down. "And the fact is I'm really busy. I don't have time to put into anything…big. I have to sell this house. There's an open house tomorrow and I still haven't cleared out the store room. And after that I have to find another place to live and —"

His brow furrowed. "Come on, that's just pathetic. I'm busy too. I have three articles due."

"I have a job."

"I have two jobs. And a messy apartment."

She opened her mouth to reply and suddenly was struck by how silly the conversation was. She giggled. "Okay you win the one-upmanship game, Zack. But I warn you, I'm thoroughly confused."

"Yep. That's pretty obvious."

"I'll try to be more open to what you're asking. You get to take the lead. For now."

"For now," he agreed. "Maybe you're right. We'll end up just almost-fuck buddies or I'll be your whatever that thing is called. Your swing back after the end of a serious relationship."

"You mean a fling?"

"Sure, okay."

"You should know. You're the one who writes for a living."

He put up his hands in surrender mock horror. "I do not write about relationships, woman. This sperm donor article is not in my usual line. I do politics. The feature articles I did about urban renewal are about as touchy feely as I get."

She nodded. When she'd seen his by-line on a couple of articles in the local paper she'd purposely avoided reading them.

But now he was charging into her life. Perhaps she should stop staring at his butt and do some Googling for his articles.

"I want to take some time with this. We'll take it slowly. Agonisingly slow. Until you're begging."

Funny, she thought she was already had begged. Her body certainly felt as if it had been silently pleading for him for hours. She whimpered again.

"So," said Zack, casting around for inspiration. "We could go park and make out in the car until the windows steam up."

She made a small noise at the back of her throat something like a sigh or whimper. Very satisfying. He tapped his lip with a finger, considering the matter. "Or I could give you a back rub. That might be more comfortable"

She nodded. "I could give you one. If you don't mind."

"Good." He rubbed his hands together. "Let's go upstairs to the scene of the crime. I want to see you on that bed again."

"You do? You said I was a basket case but you're pretty odd yourself," she said.

"Sure. You didn't know? I thought it was obvious."

She shook her head. "I've figured it out now. But no matter. I still want to—to get naked with you, Zack."

He leered at her. "That sounds dangerous. I'm not going to get naked. Maybe you should keep some clothes on too. You wearing something interesting under those jeans, like a thong?"

"No, white cotton panties."

"My favourite."

"Now I know you're definitely weird." She smiled shyly. "Or you're flirting again." Before he could answer, she started up the stairs. He bounded up after her. He couldn't resist putting his hands on the curve of her hips as they walked and he almost tugged her into his arms.

This 'no fucking' rule would be tough to enforce if she kept moving like that. Why was he trying to stay out of her body?

He couldn't quite recall the reason when her gorgeous ass swayed in front of him.

Things had changed in the bedroom since his visit three years ago. A single futon lay on the floor and clothes were shoved into a small chest of drawers.

"Going for the minimalist look?"

"The bedroom was a whole suite and Tyler wanted it," she explained. "I didn't care."

"Right. I'll ask you about that later."

"About what?"

"More details of your divorce."

"Oh. That's okay. It's boring."

He'd decide that for himself. At the moment he wanted to get his hands on her flesh. "Do you have any lotion? Oil?"

She started to cross the bedroom.

"No, let me. It's in the bathroom, right? You strip down to your underwear."

She raised her eyebrows.

"Just a backrub," he promised, though his straining cock didn't seem to believe him.

The bathroom held only basic supplies—nothing like the dens of most females he knew. Cheap soap, shampoo, conditioner, basic makeup. He recalled she'd always been uncomplicated when it came to beauty products but this seemed even sparser than his memory.

In the neat towel cupboard, he found a bottle of lavender scented body oil. The label claimed lavender helped you to relax. He wasn't sure if that was a good thing or not.

When he returned to the bedroom, she'd stripped off her shirt , bra and blue jeans. She lay on her stomach, still wearing a pair of panties.

He drew in a deep breath. "You're an obedient wench."

"I haven't had a back rub in a long time, but I remember they're great. I'll obey just about any command to get one." With a breathy laugh she said, "I really want you touch me."

She waggled her backside, settling into a more comfortable position or teasing him — or both. Too bad he hadn't told her to take off everything. The lovely curve of her butt was partially hidden by the stupid underwear.

Down, boy. But he knew there was no chance of that happening. Maybe he should have done something about his aching balls in the bathroom. Clear the decks so he could think.

He sank onto the futon next to her. Think. What the hell was he doing? His half-assed plan got even blurrier as his ability to think shrank and his lust grew. He poured some of the pale liquid onto his palm and rubbed his hands together to warm the oil up.

"Mm," she murmured. "I love the smell."

The moment his hands slid down her spine, he knew he was lost.

She moaned and writhed, arching up to his touch.

"Jesus," he said under his breath. He'd half hoped she'd be the ice block he'd screwed years earlier. It would help him stay in control, maybe even get her out of his system. She didn't want to be a part of his life and he didn't want the complication of her…but oh. Damn.

He should have known the heated kisses downstairs portended something sizzling.

His hands worked her, kneading the silk skin and strong muscles of her back. "You're in good shape," he muttered. "Excellent shape." Just the curve of her delicate shoulder blade was enough to make him want to howl.

"I hated my body," she said, voice muffled by the pillow she'd buried it in. "So I started working out a lot. I did what I could to live with it."

"Huh? Why would you hate this body? It's goddamn fantastic."

She turned her head to the side and smiled. "Thank you," she said. "Infertility."

The single word held a pain he wanted to erase. He moved to her lower back. "Oh. I forgot." He had, too. His brain couldn't retain anything but pure lust.

"I never do," she said lightly, and the words dissolved into a groan as his thumbs dug into the dimples above her butt. "Mmm." She rolled her hips.

He glanced down and saw that the crotch of her cotton panties were soaked. "'I've changed my mind about the panties," he said and hooked his forefingers in them to drag them down. "They've got to go."

She eagerly complied, lifting herself. As he kneeled to pull the panties over her legs and feet, she rolled onto her back and smiled up at him.

Obviously he'd be the only one to enforce his 'no screw' rule to their game.

He gazed at her perfect breasts with pale pink nipples, her sweet belly, her long lean legs and the dark curls of her pussy.

"Listen," he said when he got his voice back after the sight of her lithe body. "Maybe we should stop."

"Please, no," she said.

He sucked in a long breath. "Okay then we'll get something out of the way."

"Something?" She opened her legs, not wide, just far enough for him to see the flushed pink lips of her sex beneath the soft dark curls. She reached to him and lightly ran her fingers over the iron bulge the pressed against the front of his jeans.

He put his hands on her thighs. "Let's take care of that something."

She squinted at his groin. "It's not fair that I'm naked and you've got all those clothes on. That's where we can start."

He slid down the futon to get away from her fingers. "No, we're going to finish something interrupted by a few years." He bent to lick the sweet saltiness of her.

She was so slick. He pushed two fingers into the tight moist centre of her body. Dizzy with lust he rhythmically pushed his cock against the edge of the futon to keep himself from shucking his jeans and pumping into her irresistible heat.

She writhed under his hands and mouth.

"Ah!" She came almost immediately, her pussy squeezing his fingers tight. "God, oh, Zack, please, please."

The sight and feel of her orgasm almost made him come too, but he stopped moving abruptly when he realised she'd burst into tears.

She'd sobbed his name and now she lay on the bed and just sobbed.

Dizzy he sat up, rubbing at his mouth. She cried and he cluelessly stroked her leg. "Whoa. Are you okay there, Colleen?"

"You said it," she wept into her hands. "I'm just a basket case. No, really it's okay. I'm fine." She half-sobbed, half-giggled. "I guess they call it a release for a reason." She wiped the back of her wrist haphazardly across her face. Her small nose had turned pink, her eyes still shone with tears and she smiled. A beautiful vision. "That was so wonderful. Thank you. Will you please fuck me now?"

He dropped back onto his haunches. "Jeez, and they say I'm direct."

He reached out and smoothed his thumb over a tear that lay on her cheek. "I don't know. Maybe I shouldn't have...I mean I don't think it's a good idea to do stuff like this when you seem so fragile."

She turned her head and kissed his palm. Her warm mouth on his skin went straight to his already rock-hard cock. Colleen nibbled the sensitive skin of his hand. "Actually I'm stronger than I've ever been. I know the tears are odd, but really, I promise I'm strong. I want you. I could never have said that before. Heck, I couldn't even think of wanting you."

He believed her. "Yeah, I think that you've come out the other side of this infertility thing okay."

She slanted one eyebrow. "Not really. I'm still infertile."

"Well, I bet at this moment you don't hate your bod."

Her eyes opened wide. "You're right. My body is definitely not the enemy just now." She grinned at him. "But the truth is I'm more interested in your body. I want it."

"I like that you want me," he said trying to sound airy and unmoved. "Will you still respect me though?"

She laughed but he didn't.

He said, "Seriously. Maybe this is about poor delicate me and not you after all."

She laughed harder. "Tell me another one."

"Okay. The fact is I don't screw around anymore, Colleen. It just stopped working for me."

She aimed a pointed stare at his crotch.

"Oh well *that*. He's always up for the job." He waved a dismissive hand at his ever-eager cock. "I just decided not to let that be in charge anymore."

"Wow. You have changed. What happened?"

He stretched out his legs and discreetly adjusted his cock. "You happened, sort of."

Her skin still delicious pink from her orgasm, she sat back hard enough that her breasts bounced. "Me?"

She sounded so dismayed, he said, "Not really. I figured out that having fun wasn't the only point to the whole relationship bullshit. And once I starting thinking like that, 'good times only' weren't as much...fun. I'm still up for enjoying women. Don't get me wrong. But the ships passing in the night routine doesn't work for me."

She heaved a sigh. "So about the time I'm finally ready to decide to mess around for fun, you're done?"

He considered explaining, but figured there was no point, not yet.

"About right," he said and he stood up. He reached for her hand. "Didn't you say you had some more work to do on a back room? Let's get that done."

She stared at him. "You don't have to help me."

"Nope, I could go home and work on the three thousand projects around my house or finish the articles or the newsletter. Thing is, I want to do something else. Later."

She squeezed his hand and stood. "I liked the last something you planned. Will I like this one?"

He had a crude plan at last. He'd make himself indispensable. "I hope."

He watched her dress, then followed her from the room, giving a furtive sniff of his deliciously scented fingers. Christ, the hard-on he sported was not going away. He'd take care of it so he could concentrate on something other than his cock.

"Just a minute," he said and headed towards the bathroom.

"What are you doing?" she said.

"What do you think?"

"Can I watch?"

He grinned at her. "You are something else, girl."

"Well, Tyler was kind of shy."

Zack flashed on the image of Tyler masturbating. "That's not how I remember him."

"About some things. It's just that I've never watched a man pee before."

"That wasn't what I planned to do in there." He laughed. "Never mind. Let's just go clean out your room, okay?"

She gave him a bemused look but led the way down the stairs.

"I suppose we can pack. And clean," she said slowly, as if these were outrageous activities.

"Good." As an athlete he'd learn to work beyond his body's demands. He'd need those lessons now to ignore the lust still rampaging through him and actually manage to help her.

They worked on putting things in boxes. He held up an ornament and asked about it. "From my parents," she said.

He remembered hearing about the accountant and the housewife. Strict yet loving. Not so different from his own parents — minus the strict.

Colleen sat down on the floor and started flipping through some old magazines. "I wonder if I should save some of these."

"Nah," Zack said. "I can see hanging onto the ornament but not the rest. Hang onto too much and you get weighed down."

She pushed the hair from her eyes. "I can see you're not at all sentimental."

"Nope," he agreed cheerily. "Not about things."

"Didn't your mother save your first tooth, your first hair cut?"

"I'm one of four boys. I'm just glad when she gets my name right."

Did Colleen know that about him? She couldn't recall. "Any girls in that group?"

"Just one. She is the toughest of us all. She'd have to be."

"What about your dad? What's he like?"

"Dead," he said briefly. "Died while I was at college. Spring of my sophomore year."

"Oh. I didn't know. I'm so sorry." She made a face. "I remember that was my senior year and I was planning my wedding. I don't think there can be any being as self-involved as a woman planning her wedding."

"I didn't tell anyone at school about Dad's death." He taped a box shut. "And you actually were very nice to me. I got seriously drunk and you let me sleep it off in your room."

"I remember that night." She stared at him. "I thought you had just overdone the partying. I'd never seen you so drunk."

"I've never been so drunk—before or since. I held my own private wake. Remember I went home the next day?"

"Sort of." Shame flooded her. Once Tyler had finally popped the question, she had stopped paying attention to the other people in her life and here was proof. "You should have said something. I-I didn't know."

"I was all talked out. I was on the phone with my brother for hours that night before I got drunk—and while I got drunk." He flashed her a rueful smile. "Dad had been sick a while so it wasn't a huge shock."

"I'm sorry." She went to him and hugged him. He groaned and stroked her hair.

"Hey, all I needed was a place to crash that night, a place with people. You stayed." His fingers splayed against her lower back and his cock hardened against her belly.

"Tyler did, too."

"I don't want to think about him just now."

"No, I guess not." She kissed his jaw and nibbled his chin until he bent his head and covered her lips with his mouth.

"You start this up again and we'll be on the floor," he warned a couple of minutes later as his hands circled her back and reached for her butt. "I love your ass. It's perfect."

The intensity in his voice made her shiver and she plastered herself to his body, and made gentle circles against the very hard bulge of his cock.

"Colleen," he whispered in her ear. "I want you so much I'm going to go barking mad."

She kissed his neck and now rubbed herself against him as if he was catnip and she was a cat aiming to get high. God, she was drenched with lust, dizzy with need.

He drew in a shuddering breath. "What else do we have to do to get this house ready for the market?"

She froze. "You're kidding right?"

"No. Let's get back to work."

What was his problem? She could tell he was more than ready for her. Maybe he really had taken some kind of vow of chastity.

She'd respect it.

"I need to wash the shelves in here. That's all," she murmured into his shoulder hoping he didn't hear her disappointment. "You don't have to help. I appreciate everything you've done for me. Everything."

He drew in a ragged breath and disentangled himself from her embrace. "What? Are you telling me you want me to leave and miss the excitement of washing shelves? No way."

She went to the kitchen to fill the bucket with hot soapy water. He must have followed her. "Want a hand with that?"

She turned too quickly and water splashed over her front. "Blast!" She put the bucket on the floor. At least the water wasn't boiling hot and now the wet cloth almost felt pleasantly cool.

"What?" she asked when she caught him staring.

"Uh. You didn't put on a bra."

She looked down and realised her shirt was nearly invisible and her nipples created peaks in her shirt.

"I better go get another one." She turned and left the kitchen.

She thundered up the stairs and waited for a few moments in her bedroom. Would he come along after her? Dang, she hoped so. She'd stop trying to get into his pants, but she wouldn't mind if he went after her. And she'd seen naked hunger in his eyes.

Nothing happened. After a few more minutes she put on another shirt, came down and found him scrubbing the last of the shelves.

"I hoped you'd come up looking for me when I was gone so long," she said.

"I thought about it. I don't want to look too eager."

She found a sponge in the sink and squeezed the water out. "You're something else, Zack."

"Hey, don't bother. No point in getting wet again." He dumped the sponge he held into the bucket and wiped his hands on his jeans. "Done. Now you can sell this house and move onto a new life. You going to stay in town?"

She peered at the shelves. The man worked fast. She saw a couple of corners he'd missed but she'd get them later. She hated when people came along and redid jobs she'd done. "Thanks for doing my work for me. Yes, I'm going to stay in the area. I have a job I like."

"Insurance?" He sounded amazed.

She didn't bother getting defensive. "I don't sell it, and it turns out the work can be sort of interesting."

"So you're sticking around." His smile looked almost predatory. "Good."

She tilted her head and looked at him. "You want to celebrate?"

His smile widened. "That would be nice."

She tried again. Just a suggestion, no pressure. Not much, anyway. "Upstairs?"

For a moment he hesitated then nodded. "Okay."

Chapter Five

Colleen went upstairs, and this time Zack followed.

In her bedroom, she looked up him and down. "I think you deserve a reward for all your good work." Her smile made it clear she had something sexy in mind.

He went to her and, putting his hands on her shoulders, leaned into a kiss.

She closed the distance between them and the kisses continued, and soon grew deep and hot.

He stopped to catch his breath. How did they make it all the way to the wall?

"I know you've made some sort of chastity vow, Zack. But you're still up for pleasure." She stroked his cock through his jeans and his aching balls begged for more.

She made an appreciative noise in her throat that seemed to squeeze him even tighter. Still holding his iron-hard cock, she asked, "Can I return your favour? What you did for me? Oral sex. Does that count?"

He wondered how a Bill Clinton joke would go over — then decided against it. He'd just tell her a blowjob wasn't necessary and how about they go out and maybe get some dinner. But then she licked her full sweet lips and he decided he wasn't such a nice, sensitive guy after all. "I won't say no. You like that sort of thing, then?" he asked hopefully.

She was already lunging towards his belt. "I love it."

Sinking to her knees, she reached for his button and zipper and this time he didn't stop her. "Let me at him."

He watched her delicately lap at the head, then engulf it in her wide-open mouth. Clutching his cock in her warm fist, she pulled away and smiled up at him. "I haven't done this a lot. And not for a long, long time. It's fun."

She experimented, obviously not skilled at the art of cock-sucking, the tentative little touches of her tongue were soon followed by more aggressive slurps. All of it felt perfect. He groaned and touched her hair.

"Let's get more comfortable," she suggested, and pushed him to the edge of the bed on the floor.

At her first long, slow lick up his penis he fell backwards on the bed. It had been way too long since someone other than his own hand had made contact with his cock.

She lifted her head again. "That doesn't hurt?"

"No," he managed to answer. "Do whatever the hell you want. I'll let you know if it hurts, but chances are, if it's still attached or if I'm not bleeding you're doing it right."

She nodded and leaning down to suck on him as if he were a Popsicle.

He groaned an obscenity and closed his eyes.

Colleen smiled to herself as the big strong man trembled on her bed. God, the power of watching Zack mutely beg for her touch elated her. And he tasted so good. Warm flesh with a slight salty flavour of pre-cum. If cum was this tasty she wouldn't back away when he came.

This was entertaining looking at him, on his back, so hard and wonderful and large. She eyed her new favourite toy, and the craving for it thrummed through her. Would he really say no?

His hips moved, imitating fucking. She drew back and watched the thick weighty cock thrust into her hand. This was good, but the empty ache in her pussy demanded attention and here was just the object to fill it. She wiggled out of her jeans.

"What're you doing?" he started but the words turned into a groan as she went back to work with her mouth.

After one long last suck followed by a lick, she climbed up and over him. Straddling him, she hovered above his cock and awkwardly put it at her entrance. His eyes opened wide and he sat up. The sudden motion pushed her down onto him with an oof. The large hard cock slid straight up and into her. She stopped herself because it felt on the edge of painful. She was so tight, so out of practice.

"Hey," he said, propped on his elbows, glowering at her. Yet he made no move to pull her off or roll away.

She stared back, still adjusting to the sensation of something huge invading her. Huge and perfect. If she only moved a tiny bit, she'd be on the edge of orgasm again. Filled in the spot that had been vacant for so long. That had been untouched even when her husband had pumped into her. How could that be?

They sat like statues, staring into each other's eyes.

"It feels so good," she whispered.

"Oh God," he began but his words died away on a hissed inhalation when she moved her hips in a tiny circle. She moaned, her whole body throbbing with the sensation of having been seized and assaulted by pleasure although she was the one who'd jumped him.

"Should I stop?" she asked, panting a little.

He gave a tiny nod, but his body under hers ever so gently echoed her circular motion.

"Colleen, you're so bad." He moaned and pushed up as she sank all the way onto him. Impaled. Their bodies met.

"You're so good," she answered. She ripped off her shirt, then hiked up the shirt he still wore and leaned down over him until her breasts and belly pressed to him. "Thank you. Zack. Thank you for letting me do this. I need this. I need you."

He groaned and his hands gripped her bottom. He held her tight then pulled her down, harder. He might have been underneath, but he wasn't allowing her to take complete control after all. He twitched up and shoved even higher into her, so far in so she wondered if he'd come out the other side. He held her still as he circled and pumped into her. His hands kneaded her backside as he pushed her down and then almost harshly used his body to shove her up.

She'd never come without touching her own clitoris. She'd never even known she could, but as he circled under her and drove into her, the sudden orgasm hit her so powerfully she cried out and tightened all around him almost painfully hard.

"Colleen," he crooned. "Oh sweet Colleen."

He didn't allow her to rest but held her as he relentlessly pumped into her from below. The orgasm echoed through her with each of his strong shoves. Her pussy was so sensitive she could feel him swell larger inside her. Three firm pushes later, he too cried out. He pressed his open mouth against her bare shoulder and his body shuddered and jerked.

He went still. His hands still clutching her ass, gently now.

"Damn," he whispered. She dropped forward and wrapped her arms around him. She lay on his body without moving.

His hands stroked her spine and he nuzzled the top of her head. "So much for good intentions huh?"

A fast, wonderful mating, she thought. She could fall asleep now, plastered against him, if he'd let her. No movement other than their heartbeats and breath, his heavy breathing gently moving her body up and down. She rubbed her face against the T-shirt he still wore. They hadn't taken it off in their hurry — she'd only pushed it up so she could feel his skin against hers.

He ran his hand over her shoulder, down her spine finishing with a small slap on her butt. He rubbed the place he'd hit and said, "I didn't last five minutes with you, but that makes sense."

"It was fine," she protested.

"It was better than fine, woman." She could hear the smile in his voice. "And if we did it again, I'd last hours for you. Days. I'd be a goddamn Don Juan of lovemaking instead of some kind of a nervous virgin."

"Oh? Show me, then."

He wrapped his arms around her, kissed her neck and tilted his hips. His cock moved in her. Hard again? Yes. And after only a few pushes up and into her, she knew it was very hard. She held on for another ride.

But then he let go of her and, grunting, twisted his body so that he pulled out of her. She lay empty over him open and wet.

"Take off your clothes," she suggested.

"In a minute."

He rolled her over and kissed her. Now he laid between her legs, his cock rubbing her clitoris and pushing against her slit but never going inside.

Suddenly he sat up and whipped off his shirt then scrambled out of his jeans and briefs with one rapid motion.

Naked and skin to skin at last. She held open her arms and he came to her.

They writhed and kissed, long sweet kisses turning deep and awkward. His thigh wedged between her legs and she rode it.

She reached down and clutched his cock. "Now, please."

He knelt and positioned himself between her legs. Slowly, he pushed into her. His hands cupped her bottom as he stroked deep inside. One of her legs bent almost double so that as he slid inside he pushed hard against her clit.

When she was on the edge of coming again, he pulled out abruptly, with a tiny pop. She gave a wordless cry of protest.

"One last position," he said, breathing hard. "Roll over. I want to take you from the back."

"Wow you really are direct."

His eyes burned with arousal. "Fuck, yes. I want in you as deep as possible. I want you wrapped tight around me. I don't want to miss any of this. I want it all."

Slightly shaken with excitement and with his intensity, she rolled over and got on her hands and knees. His body poised behind hers — and they touched only where his fingers and cock prodded, searching for her opening. But once he slipped deep inside he enveloped her in a hug with one arm and reached around to stroke her clit. She pushed back, dropping to her elbows to brace herself so he could go deeper. He held her hips and pushed hard. His thrusts were on the edge of brutal. She hadn't known how much she wanted some mindless hard fucking. This was it.

His strokes into her bordered on too hard and deep. She loved how each one rippled through her body. Opening herself to each push, she screamed out her orgasm and arched her back so he could go deeper. Sweat rolled down her back as he slipped his hand over her skin. He clutched her hip with one large hand, steadying her, and pressed his other palm on her back. He reached to stroke her hair as he drove into her. *Animals,* she thought and wanted to howl like a dog in heat.

Another orgasm hit her like a truck, barrelling down on her. Even as she got lost in the heavy waves, his deep grunting cry echoed hers.

Breathing hard, shuddering, they fell to the side mashed skin to skin. He held her, still lodged deep inside her as he curled into her back and pushed his cock into her aching pussy, his pressing gentle now. At last, he slid out, leaving her empty but thoroughly satisfied.

She absently bent her head and licked his arm that nestled between her breasts, tucked around her. It was salty with delicious sweat. They fit together as if they'd practiced for years. "We were loud, weren't we? Like a couple of howler monkeys."

He pushed up onto an elbow so he could lean around and kiss her mouth. Just as the kiss grew interesting, he pulled back.

"Colleen," he said, in a normal voice. "We shouldn't have done that." He didn't sound particularly upset.

"Oh but I liked it."

He heaved a large sigh. "And I loved it."

She scrambled around so she faced him. She flung her leg over his hip and pulled herself close, nudged up against his warm slightly damp body. Her body felt superbly relaxed and happy even while the undercurrent of excitement still hummed through her. She was in bed with the sexiest man she knew. "So why not, Zack? I'm not diseased and you're not. Right?"

He chuckled and slid one arm under her head and stroked her back. "A bit late for either of us to ask. But yes, I'm clean."

"And it's not as if I'll get pregnant." She nuzzled his shoulder and inhaled, trying to figure out the scent of him. "Under all that sex, you smell so clean," she said drowsily. "Even when you're all sweaty. I remember that about you."

"You're kidding. Colleen. You used to smell me?"

She yawned. "In a car once. After some kind of game you'd played. Hockey, I suppose. We were jammed into the backseat of Tyler's car. I remember thinking you were the only man on earth with fresh sweat."

His laughter shook her body pleasantly. "Now that's a first."

"Unique," she agreed and he tightened his arms around her.

She might have dozed but she awoke as he gently disentangled his arms and legs from hers and pushed himself off the futon. She considered opening her eyes when she heard the rustle of his pants, his zipper and the clink of the belt.

A large cool hand rested on her shoulder. "Colleen." He did seem to like her name.

"Hmm?" she said.

"Wake up. Please."

She hadn't really been asleep but she put on a show of stretching and rubbing her eyes. Something in his voice told her she didn't want whatever was coming next. Guilt for seducing him? Her whole body felt better than it had for ages. It glowed with satisfaction. Maybe she could explain. She sat up and smiled at him.

"You've given me a gift," she said. "Thank you. I know you didn't plan to have sex but I love the way I feel right now. All achy and…and pleasant." She was going to say "all achy and loved," but that wasn't the message she wanted to convey.

"You're welcome." His radiant smile was even more glorious than the sex. Contagious too. He sat on the futon next to her and stretched out his long legs. For a several long moments they just smiled at each other. But then he broke the gaze and crossed his arms—definitely a man about to say something unpleasant. Some bad or at least serious moment had arrived. Drat.

"I didn't want to make love, but I'm glad we did," he began. She felt her shoulders relax.

"But there's a problem, Colleen. It truly can't just be this sort of casual event."

"Oh." She sat up and hugged her knees. "Sure. I'm sorry. You said you didn't do that anymore and I really should have respected you. But…I wanted it so much."

"Yeah, poor me. Tied up and taken advantage of." He grinned at her and relaxed his crossed arms to reach over and stroke her calf. "I'm not mad. I'm sad."

"Why?"

"Because I love you. I have for years." With that earth-shattering, calm pronouncement, he got to his feet. "My guess? That's why that stupid night as your sperm donor was such a big deal."

"Oh," she said. "But…Zack. It's not like you know me well enough for real love. You couldn't."

His brow furrowed, and for the first time, he looked annoyed. "Sure I could. And I know you just fine." He sounded pissed off, too. He put his hands on his hips. "You might not have noticed, but I was paying attention. You quote poetry when you're tipsy, you can't ice skate no matter how many times you try and you won't stop trying, you have two sisters and you were all over-protected, you like liquorice but only when you nibble it, you volunteer at the homeless shelter but only when it's not Christmas, you love your parents but refuse to talk about religion with them, you don't like hockey but you have a thing for the players, for years you pretended to yourself you were a prude, but you're hotter than any woman I know."

"Oh my God," she said.

"By the way, you're not the only one who from hides the truth. I didn't know I loved you, either. Infatuation, sure. But love?" His mouth formed a grim, thin line. "I figured it out about the time I whipped off your damn underpants. Hours ago. The point is, well. Never mind. But you get why I'm not going for the casual affair, here, okay? I don't want to be a sperm donor and I don't want to be a boy toy. Get it?"

He stood in the middle of her room, hands still on his hips, obviously waiting for her to say something, but her mind had turned into scrambled eggs.

"That's not fair," was all she could think to say as if she were seven years old and thwarted by a playmate who'd changed the rules mid-game.

She found her shirt and pulled it on.

He groaned and rubbed the back of his hand across his mouth. "Yeah. Sorry. I'm kind of nervous. The boy toy remark was uncalled for. Who knew love would make me an asshole?"

She yanked on a pair of sweatpants and scrambled to her feet. "You're not an asshole. I-I guess you're right. This happened so fast and we should have taken it slow."

He gave her a twisted smile. "Bye, Colleen," he said, softly. His hands lightly grasped her upper arms. "Thank you for this afternoon. Truth is, I wouldn't have changed a moment. Today was amazing. You're amazing." He quickly pulled her to him, kissed the top of her head and was gone. She listened to his thumping footsteps down the stairs. The front door squeaked as it quietly closed.

"Shit," she said to the empty room. "That really wasn't fair, Zack." This time she didn't feel as if she were a little kid. "Goddamn it Zack. Maybe you are an asshole after all."

She ran out the room and almost tumbled down the stairs. "Damn you."

She looked up and down the street and saw no sign of him. She realised she didn't even know what kind of car he drove. The fading purple sky showed the end of a long sunset. They'd spent most of the day together and she hadn't even bothered to ask where he lived.

She stormed back into the house, plunked down in front of a computer and clicked around a search engine. She'd track the bastard down.

Chapter Six

Less than an hour later, Colleen jammed on her running shoes without bothering to tie them and jumped into her car. Zack's neighbourhood was in a busy, crowded part of town and she had to park more than three blocks from his house.

She tied her shoes and ran as hard as she could. Out of breath and grumbling she banged on the door of a well-maintained duplex. She looked around at the other houses. Far busier and not as clean or spacious an area as where she and Tyler had settled. The triple decker and duplexes were practically jammed together, but the atmosphere in this neighbourhood seemed friendlier.

Maybe she was just projecting, she thought, but then someone on a porch across the street waved and called out a greeting at her. They didn't wave to strangers in her part of town.

Zack opened the door and beamed at her. "Hey! Long time no see," he said. He reached for her and pulled her into the foyer. After he slammed the door with his foot, he pulled her into his arms and gave her a long kiss.

Within a minute or two, she came to her senses and put her hands on his chest and shoved away. He smiled down at her and cradled her face between his hands for another fast kiss.

"How dare you give me an ultimatum and then march out of my house?" she squeaked. Some of her anger had died during the long wonderful kiss.

His smile vanished but he didn't look upset. "Ultimatum? No, see, I *didn't* give you one of those. That's exactly why I marched out. I figured I was in danger of pushing too hard, but I wanted to tell you how I felt."

"Nonsense. You *wanted* me to come racing after you. It was a test."

He raised his eyebrows and the corners of his mouth quirked up. "I'm glad you did come after me. But it wasn't a test. That's really not what I had in mind. I only..." He spread his palms in a semi-shrug. "It just seemed like I shouldn't hang around after I said that. I know you don't want a real relationship. You made that clear enough. So I didn't want to make you feel bad for wanting to stay cool. But I wasn't sulking. I planned to call later. Maybe tomorrow. To see how you are."

"Oh."

"Hey, I haven't declared my love to anyone before," he said dryly. "I wasn't sure of the best procedure. I know that once or twice women have said they love me and then they sat and stared at me and waited for a response. And all I could do was think, 'dear God, what do I say now?' I didn't love them—well, not like they wanted me to, and I knew it. I didn't know what to say or do. When I finally got to be the one to make the big declaration, I didn't want to do that to you."

"Oh. So it wasn't some weird manipulation."

"No, no sinister plan. No plan at all, actually. But I thought, heck, I don't want hold onto a big secret. Right? No more secrets."

She nodded. "Zack, you're too damned reasonable."

He grabbed her hand and led her from the small foyer to a sagging blue-covered couch in a surprisingly neat living room. "I thought I was too simpleminded."

A frisson of discomfort shivered down her spine. "No you're not. Who said that?"

"Tyler and some of his friends thought it. Maybe you. It's okay, dude. You're not the first."

"It's bullshit."

Zack grinned at her. "You don't deny thinking it."

The fine lines around his eyes were already deep, soon they'd be permanent. Smile lines. "You are such a pain in the butt," she said. "But listen. A few years ago, I thought the only way a person could possibly possess a soul was to have angst. If you didn't have fear and loathing, then you weren't paying attention. You were shallow."

Still grinning, he nodded. "Yep."

She moved closer to him, pressing her side against his. "That's all."

He put his arm around her shoulders and kissed the tender spot just below her ear. She shuddered and moaned. His teeth nipped her earlobe and her body quivered. Hot moist breath gently whooshed over her. "Is that what you still think? That I'm a simpleton?"

Colleen pushed away from his chest where she'd snuggled into his warmth. She scowled at him. He wasn't going to give up so she'd have to spell it out. Capitulate. "Of course not. I was the idiot. Didn't I make myself clear? I mistook sullen anger for depth."

He managed to get his arms around her again and tightened them so she was trapped in the glorious circle of his embrace. He kissed her cheek, her forehead. "I can be sullen if you want. I'll schedule a few hours a week where I kick leaves and write poetry and glower at you when you talk to me."

She blew a raspberry and buried her head against his shoulder. "Enough all ready! Don't do me any favours."

"Okay, no more giving you a hard time. For now." He released her and stood.

Uh oh, she wondered. *Now what?* Would he tell her what *he* really thought of her? He stretched his arms over his head to an impressive height. She couldn't help admiring the lines of his body. After giving a jaw cracking yawn, he said, "Hey, I'm being a rotten host. Can I get you something to drink or eat?

Of course, he wouldn't go into recriminations. This was Zack. Time to celebrate the fact, she decided. "I want a beer."

"Right and I even have one to offer. But wait a sec, I thought you don't like beer. Want a seltzer instead?"

"No. A beer."

He padded into the kitchen and returned with a glass and a cold bottle of Rolling Rock.

She ignored the glass and sipped the fizzy strong-flavoured liquid straight from the bottle. Ick. She wasn't sure why she asked for a beer except it seemed like the right beverage for the situation. He sat on the arm of the couch and watched her.

"So what do we do now?" she said after forcing down several swallows.

He cleared his throat. This was a nervous habit she'd never noticed before and she found it charming. Clearly she was most of the way to infatuation.

73

He drummed his fingers on his thigh and said, "You, um, don't want me to get lost? You're okay with what's going on between us?" He sounded casual as always, but didn't look into her face as he asked.

She drank another swallow of beer. "I'm not sure about anything, Zack. No wait, I'm sure that this afternoon with you was one of the best times of my life."

He met her gaze then, and the glow in his eyes warmed her. The heat spread to her lower belly. She shifted a little closer to him, hoping he'd do the thing with her ear again. Just thinking about it made her shiver. "You seem very clear about all of this. Tell me what you see in our future. You've got some kind of vision, right?"

He twisted his mouth thoughtfully. "Vision? Not really. I guess we'll figure out this love thing as we go along. Isn't that the way most people do it? If I feel like it hurts too much to be with you, I take off. If you feel too much pressure from me you tell me to back off. Simple."

"Really? That easy." She swallowed more beer. It wasn't so bad. Cold, too. She still sweated with the hard running she'd done. Every inch of flesh between her legs ached with old activity and a growing interest in something new.

But something nagged at her. The old miserable fact of her life lurked and she had to remind him. She drew in a deep breath. Once more, and then she'd move on. Oh, and how glad she'd be not to look back.

"Zack. Before you make all of your plans for the future, I'd hate it if you thought there was a chance we'd have biological children. Please don't forget that I can't have babies."

"Neither can I."

She felt a stab of pity and some amusement that Tyler hadn't even bothered to find that out. "Oh, no. I'm sorry. You're—"

"No, it was a joke. I'm a guy. Don't have the equipment."

Instead of annoying her, as it might have once upon a time, his flippant response made her giggle. Why not laugh at what had once seemed to be the biggest failure of her life? She shifted on the couch and pushed off her shoes so she could draw up her legs. "I wanted a family. I've grown used to the idea that it might not happen."

"I definitely want a family. But if the family consists of me and the woman I love, that's great. If it's the woman I love plus a couple of kids that don't look anything like us, that's okay too." He screwed up his face into a frown. "And actually I don't want any kids for a while. I want some time for running around naked and screwing like bunnies in heat in every room. Ever done it on a dining room table?"

She looked out over the surprisingly large living dining area. Neat, orderly, plain good furniture. A space that appeared utterly perfect for one or two people. Something was missing. She saw a coffee table, a computer table but— "You don't have a dining room table. I don't either."

"See? I better get one. So much to do before the family."

She laughed. "Heavens, you're silly. Wonderfully silly."

"Yup."

She sprawled on the couch relishing the abnormal sensation of total relaxation. "Just this morning, I wasn't ready to start anything serious. This is very peculiar. Life can't change so quickly."

"Okay, it doesn't have to be serious."

"I don't want to do anything bad."

"What do you mean? You've already been very, very bad." He waggled his eyebrows suggestively.

"I-I don't want anyone's heart broken."

"Screw that. If you're worrying about me, I've been saving my heart just for that purpose. Listen." He leaned forward and touched her mouth. "Here's the deal—"

"I know, I know. No making love," she said, suppressing a sigh. "I'd say I was sorry about that, but I'm not. Really. Not even a little bit."

"Too late for that anyway, you temptress." He slid down from the arm to sit next to her. "The new deal includes lots of fucking, making love, boinkage. But I want the other stuff too. If you can't put up with that, then yeah, maybe I'll make some kind of ultimatum. But the other stuff? I promise you it can be fun. I want to have breakfast with you. I want to do the long walks on the beach thing and I want to hold hands. And I want to bring you flowers and have you bring me flowers. I want to pile on the romantic bullshit until I've got you thoroughly hooked. And then..."

He sat back and gave her a triumphant, gleaming smile.

She quirked an eyebrow. "Well?"

"Then you can bring me the beers."

"You *wish*." She laughed outright now, gasping and trying to catch her breath. "You know, you aren't even very funny, and I feel like I'm going to bust a gut."

He growled in mock outrage. "What you talking about woman? Of course I'm funny."

True enough, she hadn't laughed so hard in ages. Not since the last time she and Tyler had gone out with him, in fact. She'd forgotten how ridiculous he was.

As she wiped her eyes, she reflected that maybe the whole strange thing with Ty had been that he wished he could be more like Zack. Maybe Ty could sense the sensual pull inside her that she'd denied. Maybe he'd tried to get her to have fun with Zack because Tyler actually cared for her and could see she was attracted to their pal. Too late to worry about now. Tyler had found happiness elsewhere. Maybe it was her turn.

She looked at the bottle she held. It was empty. "I rather like beer," she said, startled by the fact. Some lines from Robert Graves edged into her mind. "Teach me to live that I may fear, the grave as little as my beer."

"Poetry. You have a buzz on. You always were a cheap date," he said, his voice low and rough.

She wiggled her toes, and thought maybe having someone in love with her was not so bad. "Of course I have a buzz on. I never drink, Zack. Why do you want to be with a dried up old infertile bat? You could have any female. Within reason."

"I already told you. I love you," he said with exaggerated patience. "I've been with several other women and they weren't you. Good people all of them, but not you. I was even serious about one of them. I didn't understand why the hell I didn't want to marry Phoebe, and I think it's because she wasn't you. I told her I wasn't ready to settle down. Hell, both reasons were true at the time."

"Is it really that simple?"

"Yep. That simple." He got up and fetched another beer. He poured half into a glass and handed her the glass. "I was mad as hell at you for three long years. That's a long time to hold a grudge, especially for someone who doesn't hold grudges. And when I saw you in that kitchen today, just as cute as ever, completely Colleen, the anger went ppfft. Not even a shadow remained. I guess the grudge was just love after all. Kind of silly disguise, but like I said, I'm pretty new at this."

She nodded and slurped some of the second beer. "Poetic. Maybe you should write relationship columns after all."

He laughed. "At this moment, with you in my living room looking at me as if I was chocolate and you were hungry for dessert, I feel like an expert. I could write about anything in the world and be all knowing."

"Know it all."

"Exactly." He was next to her and kissing her.

Her breath went rough and fast with arousal. She was still revelling in the strange new path she'd started down. "It's too fast," she said.

"Is it? I vote we take it one day at a time, then."

"Zack, this important. I've known two things about myself for the last couple of years. I can't have kids and I don't want to get married again. I promised myself I wouldn't make that same mistake." She swivelled around so her feet were propped towards him, warding him off so she could think more clearly.

He paused then nodded. "Okay."

He pulled her foot up and put his lips on her insole. "Stop," she said. "I'm not in the mood for tickling."

His kiss went straight up her leg flooding her body with heat. Not a whisper of ticklishness.

She groaned and flexed her back. "Well, I won't think about marriage for at least a year."

He rested her foot on his thigh and grinned at her. "I said okay. Anyway, I'm not in a hurry. I'm a patient man."

She examined him. Zack the golden boy, the old pal who'd always come around when you needed a hand moving furniture, who could always make you laugh, who had a body like a sex demon. Was he going to pull her in, make her fall totally in with love him and then get bored? Or maybe this was some sort of elaborate revenge.

No, not from Zack.

All right. Fact was, despite the misery of the possible end of affection—love was worth the risk. What had he just said?

Something like he'd been saving my heart just for that purpose of having it broken.

Brave soul. Inexperienced fool. Whichever.

She raised her other foot and rested it on his lap. "I know you like mushrooms on your pizza, Zack, but golly, I don't know what else I'm supposed to find out about you. What do you want out of life? What are your brothers' names? What's your favourite colour?

He laughed. "You really don't get out much. Usually we more experienced daters do this one question at a time. Today, I think we'll answer the first. What do I want out of life?"

He used her toes to tick off his list, shaking each one *a la* Little Piggy. "I want enough work to survive, I want interesting assignments to keep my brain from atrophying and I want you. Not in that order. You. That comes first— especially you naked. Oh yeah, and world peace. That always impresses the babes, ya know."

He caressed her ankle and he dropped a kiss on her instep. His hands worked on her calf. She swallowed and forced herself to stay on topic. "Do you see yourself as writing for a newspaper forever?"

He was silent for a moment then set to work on her other foot. "I plan on taking an editing job soon, but only so I get a turn torturing journalists, too."

She wasn't sure she was ready to be distracted by the slow deep circles that his thumbs worked into her sole. Another learning experience for the day: foot massages didn't tickle her. In fact it felt nearly as fantastic as back massages. She gave into the sensation and allowed herself to flop onto the couch.

He worked up her calf, sliding his hands under the jeans. "How about you?" he asked. "I remember you were a serious student. Are you ambitious?"

She'd had no idea toes were erogenous but when he dipped his head and gave a quick suck of her toe with his hot moist mouth, she cried out and arched her back so hard she almost shot off the couch.

"Huh?" she asked when she could get her voice back.

"I asked about your future plans. Your intentions."

"Right now, I think my intention is to kiss you."

He pulled her into his arms and they kissed, in a long leisurely exploration.

"No need to rush," he murmured as he pushed his hand up her shirt to caress her nipple. "We'll go one kiss at a time.

STRATEGIC WITHDRAWAL

Alexis Fleming

Dedication

To Sunny and MisKate.
I couldn't have asked for better partners.

Chapter One

WANTED: Sperm Donor #69
Tired of humping a test tube? Sick of the sterility of the lab?
If so, come join me for two weeks of red-hot lovin' in a variety of
natural positions and settings. Satisfaction guaranteed!

Travis tossed the newspaper on the floor as his friend, Ace, wandered into the room.

"Great way to spend a lazy summer afternoon." Ace nodded to the open laptop computer on the table. "You got a deadline to meet?"

"Something the editor wants me to get into as soon as possible. It's a hot topic right now." Yeah, right, this has nothing to do with the editor. This is about having your curiosity satisfied.

Now, how to do this without upsetting his best friend? Would he want to be told if he was in Ace's position?

"Hey, Ace?" He methodically stripped the wet label off the beer bottle in front of him. "You know in college when you were determined to make your way without falling back on your family's money?"

"Yeah?"

"I knew about the deposits you made to the sperm bank." Ace's reaction to this bit of news would determine whether Travis told him the rest.

"What the fuck… How the hell did you know?"

"Come on, we roomed together for that whole year I was in the States. You live that close to a person and you're sure to find out their secrets." He grinned. "Besides, I followed you one night. Damn it, man, I thought you were shacking up with some babe. You could have knocked me over with a feather when I saw you go into that clinic in Manhattan."

"Jesus, how goddamn embarrassing. You should have said something. It was so long ago, I'd almost forgotten. I never did tell my brothers how I supported myself."

It might have been ages ago to Ace, but Travis knew the repercussions were far-reaching. "I didn't bring it up because, to be quite honest, it was none of my business. What'd you want me to say? 'Hey, mate, I know you're jacking off into a test tube. Wanna give me some of the action'?"

Ace stomped over to the refrigerator and grabbed a beer. "Why bring this up now?"

"My editor wants me to do a piece on why men donate to sperm banks. You up for an interview?"

"What's to interview? I did it for the money. Some guys made a bit of cash on the side donating blood. I donated sperm." Ace shrugged. "Nothing to it really. They just give you a beaker and the latest Playboy magazine and tell you to have at it. Simple."

"So you'll do an interview?"

"I guess…as long as you keep my name out of it."

"Have you given any thought to the end product of all that donating? You went to that clinic at least twice a week."

Ace ran his hand through his hair. "I guess I never thought about it. I was making money and at the same time, helping couples who couldn't have children the natural way. That's all there was to it."

"Not quite." Travis drew in a deep breath, hoping like hell Ace wouldn't get pissed off with him for butting into his business. "I saw a show on satellite television the other night. About a whole stack of children who were looking for their daddy. Donor Number Sixty-Nine."

"Why should I be interested in who donor sixty-nine is?" Ace made a production of looking anywhere but at his friend.

"Because you're him, mate."

"You're testing the bounds of friendship, mate. What donor number I was is none of your fucking business."

Travis grimaced. This is what he'd been afraid of. Ace getting his back up.

"What the hell makes you think I was sixty-nine anyway?" Ace slammed his beer bottle down on the kitchen bench with a resounding crack.

"Because all those kids I saw looked like you. Pretty strong genes, I'd say."

Ace's mouth dropped open. The colour drained from his face before washing back in a tide of bright red. "Me? A father? Shit, I never thought about it."

"I think you'd better. Seems like you have several kids out there, potent little bugger you are. That's not the end of it either."

"Christ, what else aren't you telling me?"

"When I was in the States last month I went to the clinic. The receptionist wouldn't give me the contact details for

Donor Sixty-Nine, but she told me they'd had many enquiries about him since the television show aired. She happened to let slip they'd tried to contact you through your old college, who in turn gave them your business number. Might be time to give your staff a talking to, because someone mentioned you were in Australia."

"Fucking hell." Ace slammed his beer bottle down on the sink. "Christ, I wish you'd said something to me back then. I might have given the idea of children some thought. How totally stupid."

"Hey, I wasn't about to bust your secret wide open." Travis paused for a moment. "So what are you going to do?"

"At this stage I haven't a clue. I can't even get my head around the idea I have one kid, let alone…"

"Hey, you'll make a killing on Father's Day. Think of all the loot you—" Travis stopped his teasing at the annoyed look on Ace's face. "Don't want to dump all over you, mate, but here's something else for you to think about. Seems an Australian lawyer contacted the clinic because three of her clients, who already had children by Donor Number Sixty-Nine, want more offspring. You have at least three of those children running around Down Under."

Ace snorted. "The clinic needs to do something about that bloody receptionist. I don't suppose she told you which lawyer?"

"Yeah, I know which lawyer. I'm working on getting the names of the children for you. I've been harassing the woman for the last four weeks now." Travis took a final swig of his beer. "You still gonna do that interview?"

"Sure, why not? Let the public know what a jerk I was." Ace glared at Travis. "Just keep my bloody name out of it."

"No problems. And just to make it a balanced article, I'm doing a piece on the mind-set of a single woman using a donor, too."

"Now where will you find a woman who'll spill her guts over something like that?"

Grabbing the newspaper off the floor, Travis opened it to the personal ads. "I've already found her. In fact, I'm meeting her tonight." He tossed the paper across to Ace. "Here's someone else who wants to be serviced by Donor Number Sixty-Nine, but forget it, mate. This one's mine."

* * * *

"Well, well, Mandy Dodds. Fancy running into you in a singles' pick-up joint. I'd have thought your feminist ideals would be too rigid to allow you to frequent a place like this."

Mandy jumped, almost knocking over the glass of white wine in front of her. Ah, crap, did it have to be Travis McCloud? "Just because I believe women should be seen as equal to men doesn't mean I have no use for men. I do occasionally date, you know."

"I'm surprised. Bet your relationships don't last long. You'd slice and dice them to pieces with that razor-sharp tongue of yours." He tapped the edge of the table with the rolled-up newspaper in his right hand.

A burst of anger exploded inside Mandy. Damn it, did he always have to rub her the wrong way? "At least the men I date have some degree of intelligence. Not like those brainless bimbos you squire about town."

"At least, those bimbos as you call them are warm and welcoming. They know how to laugh and have a good time. They don't try to cut the legs out from under a man just to get the upper hand, not like some hard-bitten lawyers I know."

She winced. Why was it people saw her as some snot-nosed bitch simply because she was a lawyer. She didn't want Travis to view her that way, although truth be told, it was her own fault. She couldn't help but needle him when they happened to meet—a defence mechanism against the hormones that went on the rampage whenever she was near him.

Even now, her heart pounded in her chest and heat swept through her veins. She could just imagine Travis crowing if he ever found out he could turn her on with a simple look. The eyes did it. A deep, dark blue, with an enticing twinkle when he smiled. Bedroom eyes designed to tempt and taunt. And the husky timbre of his voice got inside her and did dangerous things to her libido. Oh yeah, he could come park his shoes under her bed any time he wanted.

She sighed and reached for her wine. Shame he only saw the lawyer and not the woman.

"Have you decided to give me the names of those Australian recipients of the donations from Donor Number Sixty-Nine yet?"

Mandy shook her head at his abrupt change of topic. "The answer was no when you first asked," she ground out, "and it's still no. I don't betray my clients. That clinic in America should be taken to court for violating my clients' privacy."

He shrugged. "Hey, you can't blame a guy for trying."

Pushing her hair back, she tilted her head to glare at him. "Why are you so interested?" When he opened his mouth to speak, she held her hand up. "Doesn't matter. Knowing you, it's probably another story."

Travis's mouth dropped open in shock, not at her words, but at what he'd spotted when she'd moved her hair. A white flower pinned to the lapel of her shirt. Holy fucking hell, he couldn't believe it. Mandy Dodds? Sassy, smart-mouthed lawyer Mandy Dodds?

He didn't know whether to laugh or get the hell out of there. Instead, he dropped the rolled-up newspaper in the middle of the table and slid onto the seat on the other side of the booth.

"Hey, you can't sit there. I'm waiting for someone."

Without saying a word, he grabbed the newspaper and tapped it on the table. Maybe she'd take the hint and work it out. Shit, Mandy Dodds. He was still having trouble getting his head around it.

Not that he wouldn't mind getting hot and heavy with her. Something about Mandy pushed every one of his buttons, particularly the sexual ones. A rush of testosterone invaded his system, driving south until it hardened his cock. Talk about an instantaneous reaction.

He ran his gaze over her. It was the first time he'd seen her with her hair down. Usually she wore it twisted up on the top of her head with one of those clip things. Now the deep auburn strands curled about her face and softened her features, highlighting the light grey of her eyes.

Travis had a sudden desire to lean over and flick his tongue along her red-tinted mouth. Sudden, nothing! He'd wanted to grab Mandy Dodds ever since he'd met her and kiss the starch right out of her. Although there was nothing starchy about her tonight.

She'd swapped her normal suit jacket for an emerald green blouse so sheer he could see the lace on the camisole she wore underneath. That wasn't the only thing he could see. If he wasn't mistaken, given the hard little points outlined by the clingy fabric of her top, she wasn't totally unaffected by him, either. Hmm, interesting…

"Didn't you hear me? You can't sit there. I have someone coming."

"I know." He continued to tap the newspaper on the table.

"Well, don't just sit there. Get…"

Her voice trailed off as she stared at the crushed newsprint in his hand. Travis waited, knowing it wouldn't take long. She was a smart lady.

"Oh my God, no!"

His grin widened. "Got a problem, Mandy? You don't mind if I call you Mandy, do you? I can't keep calling you Miss Dodds if we're going to get down and dirty."

"You…that…in your hand." She took an audible gulp of air. "You can't be. Not Donor Sixty-Nine. Life wouldn't be so cruel to me." She groaned and dropped her head into her hands.

"Hey, it's not that bad. I'm clean, don't have B.O. — that's body odour in case you didn't realise — and I even have a certificate from the doctor to say I don't have any STDs — that's Sexually — "

"I know what STD stands for, you moron."

He spread the paper on the table, pointing at her advertisement. "You are the person who placed this ad, are you not? "

She gulped and nodded. "Um, how did…you never said anything when you first came in. What were you trying to do? Check me out first before you committed yourself?"

"I didn't see the white flower pinned to your lapel until you brushed your hair back." He pushed the newspaper aside. "Anyway, I thought you'd notice the rolled-up paper in my hand. It was, after all, what we'd agreed upon."

"Yeah and how was I to know every second man here would be intent on reading the paper." Another groan issued forth. "I can't believe this is happening to me."

"Sooo…your place or mine?"

Her breathing accelerated to the point she was almost hyperventilating. Much more and she'd pass out on him. Travis frowned at her reaction to his question. Shit, he'd had some over-the-top reactions from women in the past, but falling down unconscious wasn't one of them.

He slid out of the booth and moved over to her side. Grabbing the jug of iced water on the table, he filled her wine glass before pushing it into her hand and urging her to take a sip. "Would it be that bad?"

She took a hasty gulp of the water before she answered. "You have a terrific track record. Your children are beautiful. It's a wonderful thing you're doing, providing childless couples with the opportunity to have a family. Or women like me who don't have a steady partner but want to have a child before they get too old…"

Guilt hit him. Right about the area of his heart. He was a freakin' liar. He wasn't Donor Number Sixty-Nine. He was an impostor.

He tried to rationalise his actions. He hadn't actually lied to her. He hadn't said he was number sixty-nine, had he?

Yeah, but you intimated it. He ignored the persistent voice in his head and continued to work it over in his mind. He needed this story.

Okay, he didn't need it as far as his career was concerned, but he wanted it. Besides, he wanted to get close to Mandy. He fancied her like crazy.

He slid over until his thigh brushed her leg. A shiver trembled through her and communicated itself to him, triggering a like reaction in his own body. There was one thing he had to say about Mandy Dodds. She sure turned him on. If he stood up right now, she'd be in no doubt.

He wriggled on the vinyl-covered seat, trying to accommodate the rock-hard erection pushing at the front of his trousers. Down, boy.

What started as a way of getting a good story took on new meaning. Yeah, he still wanted to find out the names of the three clients who'd used Ace's donor gift, but now he wanted more.

This whole thing just got bigger. He wanted to get to know Mandy Dodds, because she was the first woman to get beyond his defences in a long time and he'd like to see where it went. Even verbally sparring with her gave him a sexual buzz. He had a strange feeling if he walked away from this, he'd regret it for the rest of his life.

"I don't think I can do this. It was different when it was a stranger. Someone I'd never see again after...you know. I...you..." Bracing her hands on the edge of the table, Mandy stood up as best she could in the enclosed space. "Can you let me out please?

"Maybe we should talk about this?" The moment Travis slid out of the booth, she stepped past him. Ah, shit, if he didn't do something quickly, he was going to lose her. "How about—"

"I'm sorry, just forget about that stupid ad."

She was halfway across the bar before he collected himself. "Hey, Mandy?" He took off after her, his gaze fixed on the sway of her hips as she all but trotted to get away from him.

Trying to run with a hard-on was freakin' difficult. He managed to catch her in the car park, just as she opened the door of her vehicle. "Mandy, hold on." He braced his arms on either side of her, making a cage that prevented her climbing into the car. "About the ad—"

"Go away, Travis. This is not going to happen."

"Look, calm down a minute."

"If there's one thing that pisses me off, it's being told to calm down."

Ah, Christ, he was a goner. Even when she glared at him like that, she made his testosterone rise. He wanted nothing more than to lean over and kiss her senseless.

He brushed against her. Not much, just enough that she'd feel his cock. "Make you a deal." He pressed a little harder. "If I prove I can turn you on, will you at least think about it?"

Breath held, he waited for her reply. As an added incentive, he bent his legs a fraction so the hard ridge of his erection aligned perfectly with the apex of her thighs. Then he tilted his hips and rubbed against her pussy. Heat flooded his system and he struggled to keep his breathing even.

"You game?" he managed to mutter.

"You reckon you're man enough?"

She flicked him her superior smart-bitch-lawyer look and for a moment, he wanted to retaliate. Until he spotted the rapid rise and fall of her breasts and the hand clenched at her side. Hah, she wasn't as calm as she tried to make out.

He pushed himself against her again. "Baby, you ain't seen nothin' yet."

Chapter Two

Travis rubbed the hard length of his cock against her pussy, and need spiralled through Mandy. She let out a shaky gasp and closed her eyes a moment. Hunger raged through her blood as sensation bombarded her. He'd pushed her skirt up to her hips and the only thing between them was his dark trousers and the silky fabric of her panties. Panties that were now damp from the moisture flooding her core. The warm air of a Sydney summer brushed against her exposed legs, adding to the sensations overwhelming her.

"Oh God, we ca-can't do this," she stuttered. The scourge of the law courts and she could hardly sting together a sentence.

"Woman, you all but dared me to prove my manhood. You think I'd walk away from that?" He straightened, pulling her closer, one long leg sliding between her thighs.

At the added pressure, her clit gave an insistent throb. A groan feathered across her lips. When he shifted his leg a fraction, a shudder rippled down her spine, the breath caught in her throat. God help her, he'd hardly touched her and she was about to combust.

She dared a look at his face, expecting to see a smug grin. Instead, his eyes were hooded, his smile appealing in a little-boy-lost way. Where was the arrogance he normally heaped on her head?

"Let yourself go. What have you got to lose?" he whispered, lowering his head to brush his lips against hers.

Only her self-esteem if he turned her on and then laughed at his victory.

If he turned her on?

Shit, he'd already done that and with very little effort. There was only one way to handle this. Turn the tables on him. Make *him* the one who walked away with wobbly-leg syndrome.

With that thought in mind, she grabbed his shoulders and pulled herself further up his leg until the hard bulge of his engorged cock nested against her pussy. Rocking her hips, she applied pressure, gratified when he groaned. She grinned. *Oh yeah, he was well on the way.*

"You're playing with fire there, Ms. Lawyer," he growled. "You're about to get burned, lady."

He swooped and caught her mouth in a drugging kiss. When his tongue probed at her lower lip, she opened to him, gasping when he slid inside, twining his tongue with hers. She wanted to scream when he withdrew. Dammit, she hadn't finished tasting yet. But then, it appeared, neither had he.

First he drew her lower lip between his teeth, nipping lightly. When she moaned, the sound soft and needy, he swept the tip of his tongue across the tingling curve before plunging deep again, imitating the movement of her hips. His hands clasped her ass, kneading the full cheeks as he supported her weight.

For a moment, the thought that someone might see them nagged at Mandy, but as Travis tilted his hips and thrust forward, the thought slipped away. She gave herself up to the feelings clamouring for release.

Heat spiralled through her as she ground her clit against his cock, rubbing until the friction was where she wanted it. Her breathing accelerated and tension coiled tight in her belly. Hands trembling, she pulled herself closer until her breasts rubbed against his chest. It did nothing to ease the throbbing of her nipples.

Travis braced her against the side of the car and freed one hand. Without a break in the pumping of his hips, he palmed her breast, tweaking the hard nipple between thumb and forefinger. The sensation bordered on pain, quickly morphing into white-hot heat that surged through her bloodstream until it centred in her pussy. Mandy's movements grew more frenzied, jerky and uncoordinated.

"Are you turned on yet?" Travis whispered in her ear before he caught the soft lobe between his teeth. "Is this enough, or do you want to feel my cock buried snugly in your hot cunt before you'll believe I'm man enough?"

He slid his hand between their bodies and inserted his fingers inside her panties. Mandy struggled for breath. When he parted the swollen labia and flicked at her clit, she about passed out from the fiery rush of sensation.

That was the trigger Mandy needed. The tension broke as the climax hit. Her body convulsed against him and when he thrust two fingers deep into her pussy, she rode him hard, the powerful orgasm rippling through her.

When the last of the spasms faded, she hung in his arms like a limp dishrag. She didn't even have the energy to lift her head from his shoulder.

"You okay?"

"Oh yeah." She sucked in a deep breath, her libido rearing up again at the scent of hot male and spicy aftershave. Her clit throbbed in response. Holy crap, she couldn't believe how much she wanted this man. One thought filled her mind – throw Travis McCloud on the ground and fuck the daylights out of him until he cried for mercy.

Travis slid her down until her feet touched the ground. Mandy's legs felt like wet noodles, the ability to stand deserting her. She grabbed at the doorframe as her ass hit the vinyl-covered front seat of her vehicle. Legs sprawled, she sat and stared at him.

Shaking her head, she tried to gather her scattered wits. Shit, what had she done? She'd just dry humped Travis McCloud. Oh my gawd, she'd come on to him like a randy teenager. For crying out loud, dogs went around dry humping each other, as well as any unsuspecting leg that happen to be convenient. And she'd been planning to send *him* away with wobbly legs?

The irony of the situation hit her. Dry humping...dogs...and convenient legs. A gurgle of laughter built up and she had to bit her lip to contain it. Travis McCloud and his rather spectacular leg and what felt like a freakin' ginormous bulge hidden in his trousers...

The laughter got the better of her. She fell backwards into the car, gasping as the hilarity caught hold, not even feeling the hard frame of the centre console.

Travis leaned into the vehicle. "Mandy, are you all right? What's the matter?"

"Woof, woof," she barked and lost herself in another round of chuckles.

"I must be slow." Travis shook his head. "I missed something."

Mandy scooted over to the passenger side of the car. "Not for long," she muttered. Snaking one hand around his neck, she pulled him further into the vehicle. "Come here, Travis McCloud. Turn about is fair play."

She grinned as he slipped in behind the steering wheel, the act made more difficult by her hold on him. Once he was settled, she leaned over the console and urged his head down. Fastening her lips to his, she kissed him hard, enveloping herself in the taste of him. At the same time, she slid her hand down until she cupped the bulge in his trousers.

He broke off the kiss and groaned. "Ahh, you have no idea what you're doing to me."

"Wanna bet? This kind of tells its own story." She gave a gentle squeeze before ducking her head and focusing on undoing his belt. The rasp of his zip was loud in the interior of the vehicle. So, too, was the sound of Travis's breathing.

"Mandy, this isn't necessary. I think we proved we could be good together."

"No, we proved *you* could turn *me* on. Let's see what I can do for you." She tugged at the waistband of his trousers. "Lift your ass. I'm getting hungry here."

Travis needed no further prompting. He hadn't started out to let things go this far, but his mama didn't raise no idiots. He sure as hell wasn't going to turn back now. Who'd have known Mandy Dodds has this playful streak in her? Take away the fancy lawyer clothes and she turned into a sex kitten. And right now, he seemed to be the recipient of her sexual ministrations. Fucked if he'd walk away from that.

She did something to his equilibrium, knocked him off centre, and no woman had done that for a long while. He wasn't into that ever after bullshit, but he wouldn't mind a bit of one-on-one with the sexy lawyer.

Reaching out, he slammed the door of the vehicle shut, enclosing them in the semi-darkness. He shuddered, fighting the rise of testosterone as he breathed in the scent of her arousal. "God, I can smell your sex."

"Not surprising." She chuckled. "I just came on your trousers. My wet panties left a damp patch on the front of them. Everyone will think you peed yourself."

He started to laugh. Then the laughter disappeared as she freed his cock and wrapped her hot little hand around the length of it. Within a heartbeat, he forgot the cold vinyl beneath his ass. Forgot he was in a parking lot with his dick hanging out for the entire world to see if they happened to glance in the window.

Instead, he focused on the rush of heat invading his blood. The feel of Mandy's fingers as they caressed the length of his cock before curving around the head and sliding down to the base again.

He fought to say something witty but couldn't manage it. Maybe the old saying was correct. A man's brains were in his balls. He'd heard many a woman say it, but this was the first time he figured it might be true, because rational thought had totally deserted him.

She grinned up at him. "You like that, Travis?"

He nodded his head like an idiot. Fuck, he was tongue-tied, like a teenager with his first girl.

"Then you're going to love this even more."

Travis groaned as she dipped her head and disappeared below the level of the dash. Her hot breath scorched the supersensitive skin of his lower belly. His muscles contracted. Nerve endings sizzled. He didn't believe it was possible, but his cock hardened even more.

Anticipation spiked as he waited for her to take him in her mouth, but her hand continued to slide up and down, exerting a slight pressure. Much more and he'd blow his load before he even got to first base.

"Christ, I'm dying here." He wasn't surprised when his voice came out as a husky growl. He was losing it. Big tough journalist and he was about to start whimpering if she didn't get on with it.

She buried her head even further into his lap and then he felt it. One hand still working his erection, she cupped his balls with the other. *And licked him.*

Not his cock. That was pretty standard for this type of activity. No, she licked his balls. Swirled her tongue around them before licking them all over. Fucking hell, she was treating his family jewels like an ice cream. And he loved every damn bit of it. It was so freakin' erotic, it blew his mind.

Heat slammed into him. His hips bucked, and his hard cock pulsed in her hand. He gasped, unable to catch his breath. Who needed to breathe anyway?

"Fuck, Mandy, you're driving me crazy, but I want to be inside your mouth. I want to feel your hot little tongue on my cock." He tangled his hands in her hair in an effort to manoeuvre her head — and mouth — where he wanted it.

Her tongue stopped flicking at his balls and started probing at the slit in the swollen head of his cock. She took him into the wet warmth of her mouth and his breath strangled in his throat.

Travis didn't think he could hold it together much longer. The muscles in his gut pulled tight and his balls grew hot and heavy. Hips pumped as she played her mouth up and down the length of his shaft, taking him deeper with every movement. She started to suck and he felt his balls tighten even more.

Enough!

"Stop! I'm gonna come."

Her only response was to suck harder, her hand squeezing his balls. Travis lost it. The climax hit him like a roaring freight train and he shot his cum down her throat. The air left his chest in a loud whoosh and he found himself panting like a dog.

Body shaking, he rested back against the seat, trying to recover his equilibrium. Mandy lifted her head and grinned, her wet tongue licking at her lips as if savouring a banquet.

"Hmm, nice," she whispered. "Salty and spicy all at the same time."

Travis has indulged in oral sex on numerous occasions, but this was the first woman who was happy to swallow his cum. It made him feel...special. As if he meant something to her, beyond just another blowjob. Or in his case, a walking, talking, sperm-toting receptacle.

He'd started this as a means of acquiring a story. He'd had no intention of getting intimate with Mandy Dodds. Sweet talk her a bit, get the info he wanted and back out of the deal. Now he wasn't so certain he wanted to walk away.

"So, Travis McCloud, aka Donor Number Sixty-Nine, you reckon you can handle this? I think we *both* proved we're compatible—at least when it comes to sex. Want to give it a shot?"

"Ah, I...um..." Travis cleared his throat and tried to get his thoughts in order. He knew he should walk away, but he wasn't going to. Suddenly, learning more about Mandy Dodds seemed the most important thing in the world. "Yeah, I'm game if you are."

"Well, you've already proved how determined those little sperm of yours are. And according to the clinic in Manhattan, you were in perfect health. No genetic problems a potential mother should know about."

She turned sideways in the passenger seat and stared at him. "How about since then? What have you been up to since you last donated to the clinic?"

For fuck's sake, he was thirty-seven years old. What did she want? Chapter and verse on every woman he's ever screwed? "I'll have you know I have never had unprotected sex in my life."

"Good. Are you prepared to sign a contract? I don't want any misunderstandings later, like maybe an irate daddy coming round demanding visitation rights to the child."

Shit, she sounded like a lawyer again and damned if it didn't turn him on. What the hell was wrong with him? He was acting as if he was pussy-whipped. He was about to tell her no way was he signing anything legal when he realised he'd already held his hand out and she'd slapped a sheet of paper and pen into it. Crap, his body was doing the talking for him. But if this is what it took to get close to her —

He was supposed to be the one putting *her* on the spot and she'd reeled him in as nice as any wet fish. And he *was* wet — wet behind the ears for contemplating this, all for the sake of a story. Something told him he'd live to regret it.

After he'd signed it, Mandy jumped out of the vehicle and ran around to wrench open the driver's door. "We'll start tomorrow. You can come over at six o'clock. I should be home by then."

He slid out of the vehicle and closed the door after she'd seated herself.

"And don't be late."

"Yes, ma'am," he muttered as he took a shaky step away from the car. His legs felt like chunks of jelly. He stiffened his knees. "I'll be there."

Hell, he was right. Pussy-whipped, that's what he was. He stumbled as he turned to cross the parking lot to his own vehicle.

"Hey, Travis?"

He spun back to face her. "Yeah?"

"Problem with your legs?"

* * * *

Travis pulled his overnight bag from the rear seat of his vehicle and slammed the door. Leaning one arm of the roof of the car, he stared at the house he'd pulled up in front of. The curtains twitched in the front window and he grinned. She was waiting for him.

Excitement zapped along his veins, bringing with it a rush of testosterone that flooded his system. His jeans tightened across his crotch as his cock hardened with need. He grimaced and tried to adjust his clothing.

Hell, he'd turned into a raving sex maniac. He'd been in a state of semi-arousal ever since last night. Having Mandy deep-throat him had been incredible.

Incredible?

What a wishy-washy word to describe something so fantastic it had kept him awake for most of the night. He shook his head and trudged up the path to her front door, silently reminding himself he had a job to do.

Mandy opened the door before he could knock. He frowned and indicated her business suit. "Am I too early? You look like you only just got home from work."

"No, it's fine. Just running a little late." She waved him inside.

Travis flicked a quick glance around at the main living area. It looked like Mandy. Neat and tidy, in keeping with the super-organised, no-nonsense legal face Mandy presented to the world.

Before she could object, he gave her a quick peck on the cheek. "Where do I put this?" He held up his overnight bag.

"Why do you need that? You're not—"

"I can't live in the same clothes for two weeks." He grinned. "The jocks and socks will get a tad smelly. I'm sure that'd be a big turn-on."

She backed away, hands held in front of her. "Uh-uh, no way. Nobody said anything about you actually living here."

He frowned. "Your ad said two weeks of loving, didn't it? It didn't say two weeks, but only on call. Shame on you. You're a lawyer. You should know all about false advertising."

Hah, got you, Mandy Dodds. No way you can back out of this now.

"Anyway, isn't it a bit difficult to do the job properly if I'm not staying here? Don't you have to take your temperature several times a day, or something like that? And do the deed at the optimum moment in order for my little tadpoles to have the best chance of swimming upstream to find—"

"Enough, already!" She ran her hand through her hair, knocking the clip askew. "Okay, you can stay...for the moment. The spare room's at the end of the hallway."

If he'd had a choice, he'd have opted for *her* bed, but he'd take what he could get at this point. Better not to push too hard to start with. He'd ruffled her feathers enough for the moment. He grinned slightly at the rosy stain high on her cheeks.

Her breathing had sped up and the telltale outline of her nipples showed against the fabric of her light summer jacket. If he didn't miss his guess, her libido had skyrocketed, right along with his.

Pasting an innocent look on his face, he held up his bag again. "I'll go and put this away, shall I?"

"Yeah, you do that," she muttered and walked off in the opposite direction.

He chuckled at her grumpy reply as he went in search of his bed — his lonely bed — but hopefully, not lonely for long.

Chapter Three

"How freakin' wrong is that?" Mandy slammed the saucepans around, looking for one large enough to cook the spaghetti. "The man walks into the house and I cream my panties."

She gave up on the pot. To hell with it. There were frozen microwave meals in the freezer. That would do. Leaning against the counter, Mandy crossed her arms over her chest, cradling her breasts. Damn, they felt as if they'd swollen two sizes since Travis had walked through the door. She brushed one hand against her hard nipple, gasping as sensation shot from her breast, down her body, to find a home between her thighs.

Mouth dry, pulse jumping, she pressed her thighs together and tried to find some relief from the steady throb radiating from her clit. Hell, she was a basket case.

Hearing a noise in the hallway, she straightened and reached for the sealed container on the breakfast bar. As Travis entered the kitchen, she lifted the sterilised jar out and grabbing the magazine sitting beside it, shoved them both at him.

"What's this?" He frowned and flipped the magazine over to read the front cover.

As his eyes widened and a shocked look spread across his face, Mandy held her breath.

"A magazine full of naked women's pictures and a beaker?" He glared at her. "Am I reading this right? You want me to—"

She nodded so rapidly it felt like her eyes were rolling around in her head. "Yes, I want you to."

Not giving him a chance to muster his arguments, she turned him around and pushed him up the hallway to his bedroom. Opening the door, she propelled him inside.

He shook his head. "You want me to jack off in this glass container? Is that what you're asking?"

"Just read the mag and...do what comes naturally to you guys." She edged towards the door.

"I don't believe it. Next you'll be telling me you've got a turkey baster in the kitchen and you plan on using it to shoot my sperm up into your—"

"I'll go have a shower while you get the job done. I'll...ah...I'll see you soon."

Mandy beat a hasty retreat to the bathroom, slamming the door shut behind her. "Oh my gawd, I am such an idiot. This guy pushed every button I have—plus a few I didn't know I owned—and I make him jerk off into a freakin' sterilised jam jar."

With a disgusted snort, she stripped off her suit and underwear and tossed them into the clothing hamper. Flicking on the shower, she adjusted the knobs until she had the temperature where she wanted it and the spray needlepoint in the hope it would ease the ache in various throbbing parts of her body.

With a sigh, she stepped into the glass-enclosed shower. A groan escaped as the hard needles of warm water hit her breasts. Her nipples tingled and tightened. Sensation shot through her body as if a charge of hot electricity had zapped her.

She tweaked one nipple and the feeling intensified, making her squirm. Running the other hand down her stomach, she slid it between her thighs, separated the swollen lips of her vulva and rubbed her clit, the seat of the constant throb that had started the moment Travis walked into her house. A breathy moan tumbled from her lips. She was so damn hot, if she didn't find relief soon she'd explode.

A glance in the mirrored squares pasted on the only wall in the shower that wasn't glass showed a woman with a hungry, frustrated look on her face, hair dripping around her face, hand buried between her legs. The individual squares broke up the image, but it was still enough to raise Mandy's libido another notch. She turned towards the mirrored wall and rested her head against the glass behind her, watching the expression on her face as she pleasured herself.

Suddenly, the mood was broken. The shower door slid open with a loud crash.

"Now listen here, lady. Your ad specified *natural positions*. Sticking my cock in a glass jar is *not* natural."

Mandy jumped and jerked her hands from her body. She was panting when she spun to face an enraged Travis. Her gaze travelled from the glass container in his hand to the red flush on his face, lips tightened into a straight line. Then down his naked chest to the jeans hanging off his hips, zip undone.

"Are you listening, Mandy?"

Nope. She was too busy ogling the wide expanse of chest and the perfectly delineated muscles just waiting for the swipe of her hungry tongue. Her body was already primed for sex. Seeing Travis like this simply upped the tension another notch.

Travis dropped his gaze to her chest and her nipples peaked even more. Her hands twitched and she made a move to cover her lower body. Then she stilled. Damn it, she wasn't going to act like an outraged virgin. This was *her* bathroom and no one had invited him in.

"You have a problem, Travis?"

He reached over and placed the glass jar on the vanity top. "No, but *you* sure do if you think I'm going to be a party to this."

Without a by-your-leave, Travis stepped into the shower enclosure, jeans and all. Mandy backed up, her mouth going dry at the determined look on his face. Her shower was bigger than normal, definitely wide enough to hold two people, but right now she felt crowded.

"What the hell do you think you're doing?" She moved backward until her butt hit the glass panel behind her.

"Didn't we have a conversation about false advertising?" He rested his hands on the glass, caging her in. "Hmm, I'm sure we did. People sue for something like this. Promise it all and deliver nothing. Wouldn't do for a lawyer to have that type of stain on her record."

Mandy's heart pounded. Her pulse galloped. She had to swallow twice before she could even think about speaking. "Um, I've been th-thinking." Her voice broke and she cleared her throat and started again. "We should talk about this a bit further. About what will happen after we...I...ah, damn."

She dragged in a shaky breath. "Travis, we see each other in social circles. We're in contact over certain stories in the press, issues to do with my job. I'm sorry, but I don't think it's going to work. I think—"

"Woman, you think too much."

He leaned in close, lowering his head towards her. Mandy kept her eyes open until she could no longer focus. His heat reached out to her. Her nose twitched at the scent of wild male and spicy aftershave. A heady aphrodisiac. And he still hadn't kissed her.

Despite her protests and her attempts to back out because of problems that may occur afterward, she acknowledged she wanted Travis McCloud with a ferocious hunger she hadn't experience in a long while.

Why was she fighting it? Was she waiting for Travis to make the decision so it was taken out of her hands? If so, she was an even bigger coward than she'd thought. She'd always taken care of her own sexual needs, but Travis had rocked her safe little world.

The moment for thinking was past. Travis swooped. His mouth claimed hers. He nibbled at her bottom lip before soothing the slight sting with the tip of his tongue. When she gasped, he slid inside, his tongue stabbing and teasing. She met his sensual attack, twining her tongue with his, sucking him deeper until he groaned into her mouth.

Travis broke off the kiss with one final sweep of his tongue across her lower lip. "Lady, we have something going here and I'm not about to waste all this sexual tension on a freakin' glass jar."

He rested his weight against her, his body brushing hers. Mandy squirmed and the dark hair on his chest abraded her throbbing nipples. When he cupped one breast in his hand and tweaked the hard tip already sensitised from her own ministrations, heat shot down to her core.

She struggled to find her voice. "All this is nothing but talk, Travis McCloud. What are you going to do about it?"

"What would you like me to do about it? I'm your willing slave. You name it and you've got it."

A sexy smile curved his lips. It promised everything...and nothing. Because Mandy knew darn well he was waiting for her to put it into words. Damn him, he wanted her to beg.

A shiver tracked down her spine as a Machiavellian idea seared her brain. Did she have the guts to carry it through? She stared at the knowing look in his eyes, his brows raised in question.

Damn right she did!

Pushing him back, she turned so she faced the wall of mirrored squares. The smile disappeared from his face and a frown took its place. She dragged it out a few minutes longer before pointing at the floor of the shower.

"Take off those wet jeans and get down on your knees, slave."

"Huh?" Travis shook his head.

Mandy fought to keep her face straight and her voice whip-sharp. "On your knees, slave, and service your mistress."

Travis didn't take long to get the picture. Within minutes, he'd peeled the soggy jeans down his long legs. He kicked the pants into the corner of the shower and turned to face her.

Oh thank you, God. Travis was definitely into the fantasy, given the state of the rampant erection jutting out from the dark pubic hair at the apex of his thighs.

The rest of him wasn't bad either. A broad chest with a smattering of dark hair trailing in a fine line down his stomach. Washboard abs that made a girl want to run her hands across his torso. And what she could see of his ass in the mirror squares? Damn, she did like a guy with a tight butt. Before she could take in any more, Travis slid down onto his knees.

"What is it my mistress desires of me?"

Mandy grinned. Damn it, she'd always wanted to say it, but had never had the guts before. By God, this time she'd do it. "Eat me, slave."

Travis's face went blank for a moment before a sexy grin curved his lips. "Your wish is my command."

Oh yeah, Travis was into fantasy play.

"Lean back against the glass."

When she'd complied, he lifted her right foot and licked at her toes. "Such dainty feet. You know, I can usually tell how a woman is feeling by looking at her feet."

"Yeah right. Talking toes."

Her foot resting on one hand, he slid the other up the back of her calf to the soft skin behind her knee. Light strokes. Feather-soft. But in their wake, they left tingling nerve endings. Heat zapped along her veins and her toes curled under.

"How about I tell you what you're feeling right now?" Travis grinned up at her.

Mandy struggled to come up with a smart answer, but she lost the ability for coherent speech when Travis skimmed his fingers up the inside of her thigh. She sucked in a shaky breath, waiting for him to go the final few inches. He didn't, and she released the air in her lungs with a loud whoosh.

"Is this what my mistress desires?"

He started at her ankle again, licking his way up her leg. Every so often he'd stop and nibble, soothing the slight sting of his bite with a lap of his tongue. Mandy had never been into biting, but damned if it didn't make her even hotter.

"For crying out loud, Travis, what's taking you so long? I'm going crazy here."

She grabbed hold of his hair and tried to pull him closer to her pussy. He retaliated by sucking the sensitive flesh of her inner thigh between his teeth.

Heat slammed into her. Tremors slid up and down her spine. The muscles in her legs quivered and Mandy tightened her grip on Travis's hair to prevent herself slithering down the wall and onto the wet tiles. Before she regained her equilibrium, Travis balanced her foot on his shoulder.

"Let your knee drop out to the side," he whispered in a husky voice. "I want to be able to see you." He flicked a glance over his shoulder at the mirrors behind him. "Look at yourself, Mandy. How sexy is that?"

Mandy glanced at her image. She seemed...different. It wasn't just that her body was open to view. It was the look on her face. Hungry. Eyes heavy-lidded. A flush colouring her cheeks. But most of all, she looked excited. A wave of embarrassment hit her and she flicked her glance away.

"No, keep watching. I want you to see yourself as I see you."

Travis buried his head between her thighs. His hot breath feathered across the swollen lips of her pussy. When he parted her and flicked the tip of his tongue across her clit, sensation rocketed through her.

"Oh my gawd," she whispered. She squirmed in his hold, but she couldn't escape the delicious torment. Travis played her like a musical instrument—stroking, caressing, coaxing a keening sound from her when he sucked at her clit.

The woman in the mirror rolled her head from side to side. Needy, breathy sobs tumbled from her lips. A flush highlighted both cheeks.

Mandy bit her lip at the reflection. She looked so abandoned. Wanton. But she also looked...desirable. Sexy.

And the idea of watching herself turn into a molten mass of heated hormones drove the tension higher.

A gasp escaped as Travis suddenly slid his tongue deep into her pussy. Her internal muscles clenched. Her gut tightened as the pressure built.

She tilted her pelvis forward as he pushed her leg wider, opening her up to the full ministrations of his mouth. Her hips took up the rhythm, matching the thrusting of his tongue. While his mouth continued to feast on her, Travis slid his hand between them and lightly pinched her clit between thumb and forefinger.

Pleasure slammed into her. A white-hot burst of sensation. Mandy screamed out, her voice thin and reedy. Sexual energy rushed along her veins, firing synapses all over her body like exquisite miniature detonations. She tried to hang on, wanted to prolong it, but the feelings spiralled out of control.

The scent of her arousal surrounded them, the musky aroma intensified by the heated atmosphere. The smell acted on Mandy's senses, pushing her into a cataclysmic explosion. Her body convulsed, tightening the internal muscles of her pussy, the convulsions spreading out until they encompassed her whole body.

Before the last spasm faded, Travis dropped her leg from his shoulder and stood. Mandy was barely conscious of him gripping the cheeks of her ass and lifting her. By sheer instinct, she curled her legs around his hips and locked her ankles.

She was still struggling to catch her breath when he drove home, burying his hard erection in her throbbing pussy. Oh yeah, now *this* she was definitely conscious of.

Sensation layered on sensation. Her muscles stretched to accommodate his width. Fire whipped through her blood, coalescing into a raging inferno between her thighs. Clinging tight to his shoulders, she ground her pelvis against him, driving his cock deep. At the added friction on her sensitised clit, her breathing fragmented and she started to pant.

Travis groaned and lifted her higher so only the head of his cock was inside her. Then he held still, dragging in a shuddering breath.

"Oh God, don't stop." Mandy shook so much, if he hadn't been holding her she was sure she would have disintegrated all over the bathroom.

"Tell me what you want."

"Damn you, Travis, you know what I want." Mandy tightened her grip on his shoulders and tried to exert enough pressure to push him deep again.

"Tell me what you want, lady. Give me the words."

"I want you to fuck me. Now!" At her use of the common euphemism for making love, a shiver trembled through him. Mandy felt it through the intimate connection of their bodies.

"Now tell me who you're fucking," Travis growled in a gravelly voice.

It took a moment for Mandy to make sense of what he wanted. Hell, there was only one man in the room. Who the heck did he think she was fucking? Then the penny dropped. He wanted to know whether she saw him just as a donor, or something else. Maybe the man was sick of being known as Donor Number Sixty-Nine.

"Travis McCloud!" She tilted her hips, pushing his rock-hard cock a further inch inside her. "If you don't fuck the hell out of me right now I'm going to crawl out of here and find someone else to do the job."

Mandy didn't get time to say anything else. Travis tightened his grip on her hips and slammed her down hard, impaling her on his rigid cock. A startled cry broke from her lips at the sensation of fullness. She clenched her muscles around him, tightened her arms about his neck and prepared to enjoy the erotic ride.

Travis braced her against the glass wall of the shower, lowering his head to take her mouth in a heated kiss as he pumped his hips and ground his pelvis against hers. With every thrust of his tongue, he drove his cock into her pussy, rotating his hips to vary the sensation.

Tension coiled low and heavy in the pit of her stomach. Mandy knew she wasn't far off coming again, but this time she wanted Travis with her. She felt his muscles bunch and tighten. He cried out her name and pulled her down hard, burying his cock to the hilt in her core. As he emptied himself deep inside her, it triggered a similar response in Mandy and she screamed into her climax.

Her release rocked her. Empowering and shattering at the same time. She felt she'd lost touch with reality, that she hung suspended somewhere between a blazing world of molten-hot emotions and the total blindness of a whiteout.

"Holy crap," Travis muttered. "Talk about an explosion."

"Tell me about it!" Explosion was an understatement. She felt totally worn out. She didn't even have the energy to drag her arms from Travis's neck or uncurl her legs from his hips.

"I've heard of screwing someone's ass off, but I think you did my legs in this time." He backed up and started to slither down the mirrored wall of the shower, Mandy still clutched tight in his arms.

"Wobbly leg syndrome," she retorted with a grin.

"Huh?"

"Doesn't matter." She didn't have the energy to explain the joke right now.

Travis completed his descent and Mandy found herself cuddled in his lap on the floor of the shower, the water still pounding down on them. Thank heavens she had a large, hot water supply, otherwise she may well be taking a cold shower right now.

Come to think of it, a cold shower mightn't be a bad thing. Considering the magnitude of the climax she'd just experienced, she shouldn't want Travis again so soon, but she did. He was like a fire in her blood and had been ever since she'd first run into him.

He leaned his head up against the mirrored tiles and let out a gusty sigh. "Man, I am burned out. Lady, you are amazing. Under those fancy straight-laced lawyer suits you favour, there's a volcano lurking."

"You complaining?" She rested her head against his chest and lazily stroked her hand down his arm.

"Not on your life." He paused a moment. "Ah, you do realise something, don't you?"

"Hmm, what's that?"

"We didn't use protection. There just might be another donor special on its way."

Mandy sucked in a quick breath as the reality of the situation hit her. Okay, so she knew it was too early yet, but it *was* possible she was on the way to being pregnant. Right now, Travis's little tadpoles could be swimming upstream to complete the deed.

For a moment, Mandy felt a shaft of fear. Was she ready for this? To be a mom? This was, after all, what she wanted. But at the same time, she realised just what a responsibility it was. A scary prospect, being totally in charge of shaping a new life.

The fear passed and a warm feeling settled in the pit of her belly. She grinned and slid one hand across her stomach. A child running around would please her no end. And not just any child. Travis's child.

The truth suddenly hit her. She didn't just want to use Travis as a sperm bank. She wanted him in her life for a lot longer than it would take to make a baby. Freakin' hell, when had that happened?

"You okay?" He titled her backward and stared into her face. "You really want a child?" When she nodded, he continued. "I have a proposal to put to you."

He placed a finger across her lips as she opened her mouth to speak. "No, let me finish. It's as if I've been at boiling point ever since I met you. One moment I wanted to wring your neck. The next I wanted to screw you senseless. But it's more than that. I want the chance to get to know you. To see where this goes. How do you feel about that?"

"You make a good argument." She grinned. "You should have been a lawyer, but you still haven't told me what the proposal is."

"How about we do this the natural way? Spend time together. Go on a few dates. Have some fun while we learn all about each other. If we concentrate less on making a baby and more on making a relationship, we both might be pleasantly surprised."

She frowned at him. "You're going to start wearing a rubber? Hell, that's like having a shower with a raincoat on."

Travis burst out laughing. "It needn't be, if the foreplay is inventive enough. And it takes the pressure off us both to perform. We can just enjoy ourselves for the moment."

He pressed his hips against her ass and Mandy felt the beginning of another erection. Looked like she wasn't the only one who'd be happy with a repeat performance.

"Okay, you're on. The natural way it is."

"And no more jacking off into glass jars?"

She shook her head, more than ready to give in. "No more glass jars."

Chapter Four

Mandy turned the heat low under the pan and tossed in some bacon before focusing on the scrambled eggs she was making. Grabbing an egg, she cracked it so hard on the side of the bowl, the shell shattered and raw egg filled her hand and dribbled out between her fingers.

"Ah, crap." She shook her hand over the sink and turned on the tap to wash off the mess. "Stupid thin-shelled eggs."

Ever honest, at least with herself, Mandy knew this had nothing to do with the state of the eggs and everything to do with her own emotions. She couldn't concentrate on anything except the last five days with Travis. It wasn't just the great sex they'd shared in every natural position known to man — and some not so natural. No, this was more to do with the feelings growing inside her. How would she handle it if he decided he'd had enough?

"Why, Mandy Dodds, you've been holding out on me. Is this what I've been competing with?"

Mandy yelped and spun to face the doorway. "Holy crap, Travis, you scared the daylights out of me."

Then she spied what he held in his hand. Heat washed up over her face. Oh hell, how embarrassing.

He peered at the tube he clutched in his left hand. "Hmm, glow in the dark lubricant."

He grinned, and it felt as if her heart kicked over in her chest.

"Shame it's not dark so we can try it out." He lifted his right hand. "But this! Wow, baby, that's a big one. I'm not certain I can match up to this type of action."

"That's B.O.B.," she mumbled, looking anywhere but at the big blue vibrator he held.

"Bob?"

"Um, battery operated boyfriend. You're a big enough man of the world that I'm sure you've heard the term before." She cast him a quick grin. "And I wouldn't worry too much about holding your own against my mechanical toy. You do okay."

He slowly started stalking across the kitchen. "I do, huh? Wanna give it a test run so I can compare?" He waggled his eyebrows and waved the vibrator as he rounded the table and lunged at her.

Mandy squealed with laughter at the look on his face and sidestepped out of his reach. He kept coming and it was clear he was intent on playing. She was all for it.

She took off across the kitchen, Travis hard on her heels. Before she'd reached the doorway, he grabbed her from behind and tickled her. She was so helpless with laughter, she didn't resist when he pulled her back to the table.

Lifting her, he sat her on the edge, pushing the cutlery she'd laid for breakfast out of the way. Still waving the vibrator like a sword, he spread her legs and wedged his body between them.

Mandy bit her lip in reaction as her robe parted and exposed her pussy. Now Travis used the curved tip of the vibrator to move the garment and open the rest of her body to his view.

"Lady, I can't think of anything I'd rather wake up to than this."

She pouted. "So you only want me for my body. Damn, and here I thought it was because of my legal brain."

"Baby, I'll take you any way I can get you," he mumbled as he dropped the vibrator on the table and swooped to capture her mouth in a soul-shattering kiss.

She gave herself up to the sensations swamping her, opening her lips to allow him entrance. He slid his tongue in and stroked the tip of hers, before thrusting deep.

A moan surfaced as heat streaked through Mandy's blood, driving down to centre between her thighs. Moisture pooled, the creamy slickness adding to the erotic sensation of being totally on display for him.

Spreading her legs even further, Mandy curled her arms about his neck and pulled him closer. Close enough she could feel the rigid length of his erection pressing against her exposed pussy, the satin fabric of his shorts no barrier to his unique heat.

Travis broke the kiss and pushed her back until she lay spread-eagled on the table. As Mandy heard the clatter of the knives and forks hitting the tiled floor, she started to chuckle. Thank God he's managed to avoid the condiments.

"I *had* set the table for breakfast. I thought you might be hungry."

"Oh, I'm hungry," he growled, "but I have everything I need to sustain me right here."

He fastened his mouth over one nipple. Mandy gasped as heat streaked from her breast down to lodge between her thighs. Her clit started to ache, crying out for his touch. He rolled her other nipple between finger and thumb, squeezing slightly in time with the pull of his mouth on its twin.

She groaned and arched upward, pushing for a closer connection. Nerve endings blazed. Sensation poured through her blood. Tension tightened the internal muscled in her hungry pussy. God, much more and she'd expire.

"If you don't finish this, I'm going to do you an injury." She squirmed against him.

He lifted his head and grinned. "Quiet, woman. I haven't finished feeding here."

Reaching out, he snagged the squeeze bottle of honey from the collection of condiments and held it aloft. "In fact, I think I need a little sweetener now to go with the smooth taste of soft breasts and hard nipples."

Mandy reared up. "Don't you dare. I'll—" The liquid honey hit her stomach, making the muscles dance. "Ack, it's cold," she squealed amid a bout of laughter.

"Not for long." He lowered his head and dragged his tongue across her belly, lapping up the honey as he went.

Oh God, if she'd thought she was in sexual torment before, how much more so now? She dropped her head back onto the table and gasped as he swirled the tip of his tongue around and in her belly button. She'd never thought of it as an erogenous zone, but holy shit! She felt the stroke clear down to her pussy.

Her heart raced so much she thought she'd pass out. Beads of sweat broke out on her body, mixing with the scent of honey and the musky aroma of her arousal. Mandy started to gasp, arching her body to catch the sweep of his tongue. When she thought she could stand it no more, he lifted his hand and waved the blue vibrator in front of her face.

"Now we get to try out your toys. You ready to demonstrate, babe?"

It took a moment for Mandy to gather her scattered wits. "Say what?"

She couldn't help but laugh when he flicked the switch and the vibrator started to...well, vibrate. "No, you wouldn't... Some things are meant to be private and playing with B.O.B. is one of them."

"Aw, come on, don't be a killjoy. I've never used one, and I sure haven't been with a woman who's been comfortable enough with her sexuality to allow me to see her play."

Mandy thought about it. Hell, she always came off as if she were happy with her sexual needs. Was she ready to put it on the line with Travis?

She stared at him. If he so much as sniggered, he could forget it. He didn't. His face was flushed, perspiration dotting his forehead. One look was enough to tell her he was getting a hard-on at the idea of using the vibrator on her.

"Okay, so this is getting a little too intimate, but I don't use it internally. I use it to..." She gestured towards her cream-slicked pussy, slightly embarrassed with the whole conversation, but at the same time so turned on it wouldn't take much to make her come.

"You mean to stimulate your clitoris?"

Travis lowered the blue toy and held it against her clit. Mandy's hips jerked as the vibrations travelled through her pussy. She started to gasp, her head rolling on the polished surface of the table. Tension coiled in her gut, tightening all her muscles, both internal and external.

The first of the spasms hit her, more intense because of the manual stimulation. She fought to find her voice amid the myriad emotions swamping her. "Damn you, Travis, don't you dare make me do this on my own. I want you with me," she gasped.

"Your wish is my command."

He didn't wait for a response. Instead, he dragged down his shorts and slammed into her, a fresh condom already in place. If she hadn't been so far gone, Mandy would have commented on his surety that she was ready to play. As it was, she had more important things to deal with.

She pulled her legs up and balanced them on the edge of the table, tilting her hips to take him deep. The only sound in the room was the slap of sweat-slicked flesh and the harsh cadence of their breathing as Travis plunged into her. Filling her. Stretching her. And pushing her to the brink of another cataclysmic orgasm.

She clutched his hips and held him tight as the climax rolled over her. The convulsions consumed her, dragging him with her. He yelled out her name as he pumped his hips one last time before collapsing on her chest. Mandy closed her arms around him and held on as the spasms spread throughout her body.

When she could think again, Mandy finally acknowledged how right this felt, to be here with Travis. He matched her in every way. Once again, she wondered if he'd walk away when the two weeks were up. Or would he want to pursue this as a real relationship, not a means to an end? Namely, getting her pregnant.

Ah, hell, she wasn't about to analyse it now. Why spoil the perfect moment? She'd worry about it later, when she could think straight.

Travis grinned at her. "Christ, that was fantastic. Fucking hell, baby, we're smokin'."

Mandy sniffed. Panic filled her and she pushed Travis off her. Lurching up off the table, she grabbed for the frying pan on the stove.

"Smokin' is right." She started to laugh. "I forgot to take the bacon off. It's burned to a cinder.

* * * *

After washing off the sticky honey, Mandy stepped out of the shower and quickly dried off. Wrapping the towel around herself, she opened the door and headed to her room to dress.

The bedroom was empty and for a moment, she wondered where Travis was. She moved out into the hallway again. It was dead silent...then she heard a clicking. A clicking she recognised. *Ah, shit, he didn't!*

She offered up a silent prayer. *Please don't let it be so.* She didn't want to think Travis was underhanded enough to hack into her computer files. Damn it, she wasn't ready for this interlude to end and if what she suspected were true, it sounded the death knell.

Straightening her spine, she tiptoed towards the room she'd converted into her office. The door was wide open and there sat Travis, perfectly at home in front of her computer. He'd tilted the chair back, his bare feet balanced on the edge of the desk. The keyboard sat on his lap, his fingers madly flying across the keys.

"I thought I could trust you." She leaned against the doorframe, arms folded across her chest to hide the trembling of her hands.

Travis jumped. His feet slid off the desk. The chair dropped back onto the carpeted floor with a soft thump. "Jesus Christ, woman, you scared the crap outta me." He slid the keyboard onto the desk and angled a glance at her.

"That's evident. Guess you figured you had time to crack my files and learn the names of my donor recipient clients. I hate to disillusion you, but I don't keep my client list on my private computer. So you're out of luck." She shook her head.

"You couldn't leave it alone, could you? Once a reporter, always a reporter."

He ran his hand through his hair. "Look, Mandy, I—"

"Don't you 'look Mandy' me. Are you going to sit there—and get the fuck out of my chair—and tell me the idea of looking for my clients' names never crossed your mind?" She raised her eyebrows and waited for his reply. *Lie, Travis, lie. Don't shatter my faith in you.*

"Okay, so I searched your desk."

She bit her lip to stifle a groan. Damn, why hadn't he lied?

"Yeah, I started to look for something to tell me the names of the women, but I found I couldn't do it. I—"

He rounded the desk and advanced on her. Mandy held her ground. She didn't want him to touch her, but she needed him to realise how important this was to her. More than that, she needed the answer to another question, one that would be the make-or-break of any relationship between the two of them.

"I told you, I couldn't do it." Travis held his hand up as she opened her mouth to speak. "Yes, I searched your desk, but I couldn't go any further. I did *not* hack into your computer. I was only using the word processor to write a story, something I wanted to get off to the editor as soon as possible."

Mandy skirted Travis and stomped to the windows overlooking the back garden. Part of her wanted to watch his face as she asked her next question, but, right now, she was too much of a coward.

"Why did you come here, Travis? Why did you answer the ad?"

"You wanted Donor Number Sixty-Nine. Hey, I—"

"Was that all it was? A chance to prove your prowess? And don't lie to me, Travis, because I'll know." Now she turned to face him. This was too important to hide from.

Travis wandered about the room, lightly grazing the furniture with the tip of his fingers. Mandy had a sudden need to feel the same fingers brushing against her body. To experience the rush of heat that followed his every touch. She ignored it.

"Okay, if we're laying our cards on the table, I guess now's the time to tell you I answered the ad because I wanted a story about why single women would decide to have a child on their own, particularly a child without the father being a part of his life."

"And that's why you stayed? Because of a story?"

"Jesus, Mandy, what do you want me to say? Yes, I came for a story, but I stayed because I wanted to. You turn me on more than any woman I've ever met. Damn it, woman, we could have a future here if you weren't so pigheaded."

Mandy sucked in a sharp breath. "Pigheaded? I'll give you pigheaded." She pointed towards the door. "Pack you bag and get the hell out of here, Travis. You aren't the man I thought you were."

"You reckon? Well, I'll tell you something else for free, lady," Travis growled. "I'm not Donor Number Sixty-Nine either."

Shock slammed into Mandy. "*What*? You're not... But—"

The ability to form a coherent sentence totally failed her. She stood there staring at him with her mouth wide open like a stranded fish. She peered into his eyes, looking for the truth. Then it hit her. Travis McCloud was *not* Donor Number Sixty-Nine. She'd been conned.

Hurt bled into her soul, washing away the last of the shock. Now anger rode her, fizzing through her veins like a superheated charge of electricity. She clenched her teeth until her jaw ached. It was either that or start screaming at Travis. *Bastard!*

"Say something, for God's sake." Travis moved to stand in front of her, reaching out to rest his hands on her shoulders.

Mandy glared at him. "Get. Your. Hands. Off. Me."

He backed up, hands held in front of him. "Okay, at least let me explain."

She snorted. "Think you can?"

"I'm not the donor you wanted, but I know him. Part of the plan when I answered the ad was to try to find out the names of the donor parents for him. But basically, I just wanted a story. That ad was the perfect opportunity to get what I needed. I never intended things to go as far as they did."

"What? You never intended to fuck the stupid lawyer? My, how sad that you had to lower your standards like that."

Travis slammed his hand down on the desk. "Will you stop it? It wasn't like that at all."

He straightened and ran a shaky hand through his hair. "Okay, so I tricked you. I never said I was the donor you were looking for, but I never denied it either when you assumed I was."

"God, you must have been laughing up your sleeve at me all the time." She turned and faced the window again. "Go away, Travis. Get the hell out of my house." *Go…before I burst into tears.* Right now, the sense of betrayal was so sharp she didn't think she could deal with much more.

"So that's it? You're going to finish it, just like that?"

"Yep, you lied to me. Is that the type of man I want as the father of my children? I don't think so."

"And what if you're already pregnant? What happens then?"

At that, Mandy spun around to face him. "I can't—"

"Oh yeah? We might have used condoms for the most part, but have you forgotten that first time?"

She had. Now the memories rushed back, bringing with them a flood of heat and a sudden dampening of her panties. Shit, even her body was betraying her now.

"What if I am pregnant?" She managed a careless shrug. "It doesn't concern you any longer."

He let loose with a sharp bark of laughter. "How do you make that out? If you are and I'm the father, of course it concerns me."

"*If* I happen to be pregnant, I'll raise the child on my own. I don't need you. I did without a man in my life before, and I can do it again. It's time for you to make a strategic withdrawal before I do something I'll be sorry for. I sure as hell don't want to be responsible for killing or maiming the father of my child."

Ah hell, if he didn't go soon she'd lose it. Either dissolve into tears and beg him to stay, or start throwing things. Preferably something lethal. Something that would make Travis hurt as much as she was hurting right now.

"If you think I'm going to walk away and have nothing to do with any child of mine, you can think again, lady."

She managed to chuckle, the sound lightly tinged with hysteria. "Tough. Have you forgotten you signed a contract? You have no rights over any child between us. You can't even see the baby unless I decide to let you."

Travis moved towards the door. His lips were drawn into a tight line. Two red spots of colour highlighted his cheekbones. His eyes glinted as he stared at her. "Well, is that right? Sweetheart, for a lawyer you're awfully naïve. That contract is null and void. Go check it out if you don't believe me. I signed it as Donor Number Sixty-Nine and I ain't him."

Then he turned and walked from the room, leaving Mandy standing there with her emotions hanging out for the entire world to see.

Chapter Five

Travis tipped his head back and guzzled the last of his beer before tossing the empty bottle towards the bin. It missed. The resultant clatter brought Ace striding into the living room.

"When are you going to snap out of this, mate? I'm tired of picking up your mess." Ace bent down, scooped up the empty bottle and tossed it into the trash can. You've moped around for two weeks now. You want this woman so bad, get your ass into gear and go do something about it."

"Why the hell should I? She tossed me out. Let her make the first move." Travis pushed himself to his feet and sauntered over to the refrigerator. He reached out to grab another beer and paused. "Ah shit, I can't even get a good drunk going. Three beers and not even the slightest bit of a buzz."

Instead of another drink, he turned the faucet on and held his head under the cold spray. With water running in his eyes, he groped around for the hand towel he always left beside the sink, grunting his thanks when Ace handed it to him.

Finger-combing his wet hair back from his face, he snapped on the coffee maker. Maybe it was time for a change of beverage. The alcohol sure wasn't making any difference. "You want one?" He gestured to the machine. At Ace's nod, he dragged down a second coffee cup.

With the coffee poured, he parked himself in front of his laptop at the dining table, while Ace took up his favourite position with legs curled over the armrest of the lounge chair. "I can't understand why she cut up at me so violently. She didn't even give me a change to explain why—"

"Use your brains, Travis. You lied to her. Went in there under false pretences. What do you expect? That she'd pat you on the head and tell you it was okay?" Ace shook his head. "Don't you know anything about women? Man, you made a fool of her. You'll have to belly-crawl to get back in her good books after something like that."

"I never set out to make her look foolish. Hell, I still don't think I did do that," he mumbled, lifting his coffee cup to take a sip.

Ace burst out laughing. "Trust me, mate, that's how she's feeling right now. I'll bet my last dollar on that. Women hate to be lied to and right now she's probably feeling like you just used her to get your story."

"Well, wasn't she using me, too?" He scowled at his coffee cup as if the answers were contained in the dark brew.

"But she was up-front about it. You knew exactly what you were getting when you answered that ad." Ace joined Travis at the dining table, pointing at the laptop. "Is that your story about her using a donor to have a rug-rat?"

"I'm not going to write the story now," Travis mumbled, closing the laptop with a snap.

"Sorry, didn't hear that?"

"I'm not going to write the fucking story, all right?"

"Why not?"

Travis glared at his friend. "Leave it alone, Ace."

"Then answer me."

"Because I care," he yelled. "I'm not going to splash our private business all over the tabloids." He shook his head. "I care," he whispered, "a lot."

Ace had the audacity to grin. "So get off your ass and go after the woman. Tell *her* how you feel."

Travis shook his head again, a slight grin climbing up his face. "You're a bastard, you know that? I'm glad you're my friend and not my enemy. And getting off the subject of me, what are *you* going to do about *your* problem? It won't go away if you ignore it. It's just going to get bigger."

"Decision's already made. I'm going home to face the music. Not certain what I'm going to do yet, but I have to do something. I can't—"

Before he could go on, the front doorbell rang. "Hold that thought." Travis uncurled his long length from the chair and sauntered out of the room, Ace trailing in his wake.

Travis opened the door to a young man wearing a shirt sporting the logo of a local florist.

"Delivery for Travis McCloud," the kid said in a nasal voice, holding out a cane basket wrapped in clear cellophane paper and tied with a huge red bow.

He handed the boy a tip and took the basket inside, slamming the door with his hip. "Who the hell is sending *me* flowers?"

"Easy way to find out." Ace grinned. "Open it and read the card."

The basket cradled in one arm, Travis ripped off the red ribbon and spread the paper wide. Then he started to laugh.

Inside was the big blue vibrator with a red bow around the head. Next to it nestled a glass beaker in which resided a collection of foil condom packets. The turkey baster lay across the top, tied up with a yellow ribbon. And in among all that was a swirl of brightly coloured confetti, myriad rose petals, and a large note addressed to him.

Ace yanked the note from the basket and held it out so they could both read it.

Travis McCloud is cordially invited to a one-off showing
of the Lolita (formally known as Mandy the Moron) striptease
extravaganza.
Satisfaction guaranteed. Natural positions and settings only.
Please bring whichever toys take your fancy
from the collection included in the basket.
8 PM at the moron's residence.

"What the fuck?" Ace stared at Travis, a perplexed look on his face.

Travis grabbed the vibrator from the basket and held it out like a sword, thrusting and parrying. "Yee-haw, I've been forgiven."

* * * *

A shiver slid down Mandy's spine as she heard Travis pull into the driveway. *Nerves. Get over it, woman.*

She hadn't even been certain he'd come. He could have just told her to fuck off and then where would she be? She didn't even want to think about it and certainly not right now. Not with the performance about to start.

Unlocking the front door, she turned and flicked on the music she'd set up on the tape player before getting into position. As Travis opened the door and stepped inside, she let the music take her, grinding her hips to the sultry beat.

When she was sure she had his attention, she slowly allowed her robe to slip off one shoulder. "I'm not pregnant, you know," she tossed over her bare shoulder as she turned her back and gyrated her hips.

A grin tilted her lips as she flicked her gaze down the front of his jeans. If the bulge present there was any indication, the performance was definitely having the desired effect.

"And that makes you what? Happy or sad?"

She dropped the robe from the other shoulder. "Part of me is sad. I really want to have a child. But I've realised something through all this."

Hips bumping and grinding in time to the music, she danced over to stand in front of Travis and trailed her hands across his chest, flicking the buttons of his shirt undone. That done, she dropped the robe a little lower and angled her body so he could see her breasts were bare.

When he groaned in response, she chuckled and drew one finger down to follow the waistband of his jeans. Quick as a flash, she undid the top button. "You want to know what I discovered, Travis?"

Suddenly, she stopped all the sensual contortions. This next bit was too important to dress up with sex. "I discovered having a baby on my own without a supporting loving relationship is not all it's cracked up to be."

Travis grabbed her hand, effectively stopping her from sliding his zip down. "So what do you want, Mandy?"

"You." She let the robe fall a little farther down her arms until only the very tips of her breasts were covered. "Yes, I want to be a mom, but I want you more than I want a baby. A child should be the natural extension of a loving relationship wherever possible. That's what I want for us."

He dragged her close, wrapping her in his arms. "Thank you, God," he whispered.

For a moment, there was complete silence. Travis rested his head on hers and drew in a deep, shuddery breath. Mandy found she had to blink to keep the tears at bay. She couldn't believe it had turned out okay. She'd been so afraid Travis wouldn't come, that he'd throw her invitation back in her face.

"I'm sorry I didn't listen to you." She angled her head so she could see his face. "I guess I needed some time to sort out things for myself."

"No more strategic withdrawals, baby. We're in this together from here on out, all right?"

"You bet."

Mandy felt a momentary pang of loneliness as Travis pulled back from her, putting space between them. His lips pressed together in a tight line, his brow furrowed in a frown.

"There is one thing, though."

A sinking feeling of panic settled in her chest. "What?"

"Where Lolita? You promised me an extravaganza." He dug into the back pocket of his jeans and whipped out the big blue vibrator, the red bow still attached to it.

Mandy backed away from him and started laughing so hard she forgot to hold her robe together. Travis's eyes gleamed at the flash of naked breasts and the tiniest g-string she could find. Then he brandished the vibrator like a weapon and started to advance on her.

"It's show time, baby," he called out with another expert thrust.

Well, hell, did he really think she was going to run?

PLAYING THE ACE

Lyn Cash

Dedication

For Alexis & Summer ~ thanks for playing

Chapter One

Every intimate glance over their steaming cups of coffee in the Sydney airport bistro convinced Ace Elliott that he would fuck the ubiquitous blonde. He knew when she shared her chocolate chip biscotti with him that they'd have the wildest sex of their lives once their plane lifted off, sending them towards Los Angeles. Past that, he had no clue, because the more he saw of her, the more lost he became, and all he could pray for was that she'd find him. Ever since he'd entered the airport, he'd seen her either directly before him or out of the corner of an eye. Fated...that's what their mating appeared to be...kismet, because he couldn't shake her image. She was everywhere.

He'd first encountered the statuesque lady up close in the waiting area, when they'd all been informed their plane would be delayed by a couple of hours. Like he, she'd accepted the news quietly then walked back outside to smoke with others who preferred a nicotine fix to sitting and watching the clock. Granted, it was a pain in the ass to go down the escalator, outside, then back up and through security again, but with time to kill, it was preferable to sitting while waiting. They'd have time enough to sit for between fifteen and twenty hours in the airplane.

Her lips intrigued him — they were luscious, full, slicked with a cherry red gloss that seemed natural. She was born to wear the colour, which enhanced, rather than detracted from or washed out her porcelain skin. Every time she'd brought the cigarette to her lips, his cock had flared to life in tandem with the cherry on the end of the fag. With each exhale, his body felt a pull, his mouth the desire to capture her breath.

Wordlessly, they'd studied their surroundings like others taking a last-minute smoke break, breathing in the hot December air and watching the gulls swoop, perhaps wistfully thinking of what might have been had they stayed. For all Ace knew, she was a native, leaving home for God knew what. Or she might be an undercover operative for some Nordic-based ring of spies. She certainly made him feel like James fucking Bond, silently studying his nemesis, the woman with the power to seduce, one who could destroy him should he let her get too close.

Ace snorted as his fantasies clashed with reality. 007, indeed. *How about Agent 69*, he asked himself, remembering why he was leaving Australia.

He'd taken one last drag on the cigarette and snuffed it in the nearby receptacle. The blonde had done the same and had walked beside him then ahead of him once they'd reached the entrance.

She'd seemed to know where she was going, so she was no stranger to the airport. Ace had found himself following her, still in spy mode, waiting for her to reveal something about herself.

Once they'd passed through security, his goddess had window-shopped, seeming leisurely and pausing only when something caught her eye. This time it was a jewellers'. She'd pointed to a diamond-encrusted tennis bracelet, tried it on. Ace had watched in fascination from the opposite end of the glass counter. She'd whispered something, most likely asking the price, since the clerk's response announced the value.

Ace's curiosity got the better of him. When she'd frowned, pursing her lips and shaking her head, then walked to another counter, he'd gravitated towards the same clerk, same bracelet, and with a silent nod and the point of a finger indicated he'd like to see the item.

A thousand bucks. An expensive trinket, but not for someone like her. Her body screamed sex, and what sexier gems than diamonds for her wrist? Ace had almost laughed. He'd nodded once more and fished in his pants for the wallet holding his credit cards.

He'd cut a glance her way and caught her shocked expression then was rewarded by seeing her blush furiously. Good. He'd definitely had the upper hand here.

The clerk had proceeded to wrap the gift once it had been rung up, but Ace had shaken his head. "Just the box, please."

He'd paused at the doorway, and wordlessly, the blonde had acquiesced, walking towards him without looking at him, as if she'd tired of shopping.

Ace had never been one whose cock dared jump the gun, instructing the brain what came next. Since childhood, he'd been able to call the shots, set up the deal, wait for the other party to fall into line. The blonde was different, though. Sometimes, during their wordless play, he'd felt she was on the same page with him, allowing him to set their pace, and others, like when she'd slipped into the bathroom without so much as a by your leave, he'd felt she'd turned the tables, taking the upper hand, leaving him gasping like a fish on a sandbar, and wondering what came next, whether he'd drown or be rescued.

What really freaked him out was that there were moments when he wasn't sure who was playing who. Couldn't call it stalking on her part if she walked ahead of him, but he definitely felt like a sting was about to take place.

She hadn't spoken a word, and Ace longed to hear her voice, preferably loud enough that this time he'd understand precisely what she was saying. But part of him wanted no verbal communication. After the shock he'd had prior to leaving Oz, he wanted to remain anonymous, even if it meant the person with whom he was engaged did the same. Sometimes being clueless was a blessing.

He'd certainly been naïve when he'd sold his sperm to handle college expenses. Now, it seemed, people were after him. Mothers. First they'd wanted his sperm — now they wanted his blood. They wanted to know who he was. Why, for godsakes?

He shuddered. How many offspring had he fathered? Did it matter? Was his impractical mind still at play, telling him that all he'd done was give children to the childless? Damn the consequences, the adult Alexander Carter Elliott, whom his father had dubbed Ace, wanted to know what he'd done. He just wasn't prepared for what he imagined to be an avalanche of response once he opened that door.

His blonde companion seemed to be his last hope of a normal life, if one could call setting up a mile-high fuck normal.

Ace winked at her over the coffee mug, and she didn't wink back. She didn't even smile. He wondered what she was thinking. She obviously knew that he'd purchased the tennis bracelet. Did she wonder if it was meant for her or if he had a mistress back in the States?

He chuckled ironically and almost snorted coffee up his nostrils. *Wake up, Ace. She doesn't give a shit about you or your money. She probably has a husband and four kids waiting on her to come home, and you're just a mindless flirtation to pass the time.*

He self-consciously touched the jewellery case in his jacket pocket, but he was thrilled to find her lowered eyes following his hand's move. Maybe she wasn't immune to him after all, or to the purchase he'd made. Not that he had anyone else in his life to receive those diamonds. His mother had been dead for nearly two decades, and his last girlfriend had called him a workaholic son of a bitch for ignoring her needs and devoting so much of his time to his business.

His thumb and forefinger stroked the box, but his mind imagined the blonde rubbing his cock. Her blue eyes were round with surprise, her red lips parted, white nostrils flaring slightly. Shimmering blonde tendrils escaped her severe bun, and Ace wanted to wrap her in kisses, unpinning the rest of her hair, making love to her and eliciting moans of pleasure while she restlessly ground her pussy against him.

The government spy monologue his mind had conceived was interrupted by an announcement that their plane was ready for boarding.

Agent 69 and the Nordic femme fatale wordlessly finished their coffee and biscotti. A tiny crumb lingered near her mouth, and Ace couldn't help himself. He leaned in and licked it off, thanking her with a quick peck on the lips. He'd be damned if he was leaving that airport without at least kissing her.

* * * *

143

Her sister-in-law Jenna had been right—Ace Elliot was indeed dangerous looking, but he definitely had a sense of play if he could do the cloak and dagger intrigue with her.

Katya Grishenka settled into her coach-class seat and stared out the window. She'd spent the past four years in Australia helping Jenna get her business off the ground, and now she was going home to her adopted country, America. She, her brother, and their two sisters had moved to the States in the early nineties with their parents when they were but kids. Now her oldest sister was desperate. Elena's child needed a bone marrow transplant, and Katya was the one Elena wanted by her side.

Little Nikanor and his twin, Nina, had been adopted by friends of Elena upon their birth, but when the couple perished in a freak accident, Elena discovered she'd been named executor of their estate and guardian of the children. Single motherhood had been fine, but now with Nik's disease, the family was in a frantic search for his birth father.

"We think we've found him." Elena's voice had quivered with excitement and anxiety. "Getting the man here and willing to take a paternity test will be next to impossible though."

Before Elena finished explaining, Katya had wondered what that had to do with her.

"We know the man has worked in Sydney off and on during the past few years and that he has family here in the Midwest."

"I still don't understand." Katya had truly been puzzled.

Her eldest sister's voice had held hysteria. "You won't believe how I found him. I put an ad in about seventy major newspapers in the States, and one of the man's brothers contacted me. David."

"This David…how can he be so sure?"

"We've become very close during my search, and...I trust him when he says the children are his brother's."

"What does close mean? Is he your boyfriend?"

"My fiancé. Look, I know this sounds unbelievable, but I placed the ad, he answered, and...I don't think he'd tell me his brother fathered the children unless he himself was sure. He recognised the birthmark. Seems all of Ace's children carry a gene he received from his mother, a definitive piebald streak in their hair...and all the kids I've found have dark hair and blue eyes. You'd have to see to believe — the resemblance they all have to one another is remarkable. Same patrician nose, wide-set eyes, high brows, and chiselled features. They all look like miniature Melina Kanakaradis with dark hair, Mena Suvaris with blonde, or Yannis — without the moustache, of course."

"Now you're joking."

"Not at all!" Elena had rushed to add, "Their mother died when Ace was still in elementary school, leaving the father to rear four boys by himself. Once he graduated, Ace didn't agree with his father's plans for his future, so he set out on his own. In order to survive, he donated sperm to fund his studies."

Ace? The poor child was named for a playing card?

"Katya, please, just help bring him home. Feed the information I give you to Jenna and Mandy, and see if they might have some ideas. I hate to just drop this on the poor man, but Nik can't wait much longer, and the blood tests thus far have proven that Nik's father and David are related, so we're ninety-nine percent positive that Ace is Nik's father."

That's all well and good. Katya folded her arms and thought for a moment. *But how in hell do we get the man to agree to a paternity test?*

She buckled her seatbelt, popped a mint into her mouth to help with the change in cabin pressure on her ears, and took a nervous breath.

Katya was torn between the belief that the sperm donor was entitled to privacy and the knowledge that uncovering his secret might help several lives and grant his current and future children access to information that some of them would surely seek some day.

It's playing God, and that is never good. She closed her eyes, feeling a slight tickle in her tummy as the airplane lifted off. She should never have dared leave on the same flight. She should have left well enough alone once she'd given Mandy and Jenna ammunition to go after him. She could have taken an earlier or later flight.

His dark eyes haunted her vision, despite her closed eyelids. Moisture pooled between her legs, and her nipples tingled with false hope. No, she knew she had to see him up close, the man whose body had produced what now amounted to about fifty-some children. To think that most likely he'd never known what it was like to come inside any of those mothers, that to date he didn't know what it felt like to create life with another person…a woman he loved.

She stared out the window at the sky. The clouds that had seemed white and fluffy against a cornflower blue sky now seemed grey and ominous, as if it wouldn't take long before they were roiling. *That's just fucking great – a storm.*

Her throat went dry, and she inwardly jumped, but she maintained what she hoped was a nonchalant expression. Then she looked up.

Dark-fringed lashes above innocent looking dark eyes peered at her, stripping her of common sense, and she almost chuckled. *Don't crack*, she told herself. *Don't let him see his effect on you, and for crap's sake don't be the first to break the gaze.*

He offered her his hand to help her to her feet, and she took it, careful not to look away until her head was directly beneath his chin. She was certain he was studying her head to see if the naturally blonde roots were fake, and it gave her no small measure of pleasure to see his chest swell beneath her gaze. So. She affected him in much the same way he affected her. Good.

The plane was large, an airship thrumming with power. She hadn't a clue where Ace was leading her, but she figured it couldn't hurt to go with him. Maybe he wanted to talk to her over drinks. Would they discover the airline's stash of individualised rum or scotch, share a toast and laugh at how they'd first noticed one another? If so, maybe she could introduce herself, tell him her purpose in wanting to meet him. He might even forgive her once he realised her cause was altruistic.

Perhaps they would simply continue staring at one another, waiting for the other to crack a smile, verbalise something. She hoped so—the suspense of longing to hear his voice or just see him smile was killing her.

One of the stewardesses smiled as they passed, giving Katya a nominal glance at best, her gaze lingering, however, on the runner's build beneath Ace's expensive shirt and slacks.

Katya slowed as they came to the end of the plane. She looked about but saw no other stewardesses, certainly not a cash bar. She opened her lips to speak and felt his body press into hers as he reached around her. Too late, she saw where he'd planted his hands...on the door to one of the bathroom stalls. She whirled to speak, her throat suddenly tight with tension, her pussy wet with desire at the thought of what he obviously had in mind.

"I can't—we have to go back—oh, what if someone's watching?" She managed to eke out a few words before his lips closed over hers and his tongue slipped deliciously between her teeth.

Weak-kneed, she collapsed against him as he lifted her ass and settled her on the cold, narrow sink. She felt and heard more than saw him close the door and slide the lock into place, as surely as he worked her skirt up to her waist and slid his fingers inside her panties.

"Wet and wild." His breath mingling with hers was a seductive whisper.

Liquid heat pooled between Katya's thighs when she heard Ace's voice for the first time. She was torn between wishing he sounded like Pee Wee Herman and Barry White. If he sounded like the garish comedian instead of the seductive singer, it'd be a helluva lot easier to dismiss the sexual fantasy that had plagued her ever since she'd laid eyes on him.

Ace wet his lips. "I'll bet you taste like honey and vanilla."

Katya's head lolled back, and she drew the deepest breath possible considering her circumstances. "What makes you say that?"

"Because anything as creamy and succulent looking as you just has to taste sweet." He continued licking the inside of her mouth as he finger-fucked her. "I want you!"

She clung to his shoulders, unable to stop his hands from their exploration even if she had access. "So fuck me!" She arched her back as he lifted her once more, this time sliding her forward and onto his cock. He was huge!

She may have been wet and wild, but he was satin and steel, his cock smooth and warm, hard as sheet metal against her throbbing clit as he teased her entrance.

"You any good at this?" He handed her a foil packet.

She took it and ripped it open with her teeth, stifling a fit of giggles. She couldn't believe she was about to have sex in a latrine with the very man she'd been following for weeks.

He took the condom from her once she had it out of the packet and rolled it onto his cock, kissing her the whole time. When he was done, she gasped as his fingers opened her pussy's tender lips, priming her. His fingers were so sure and strong, rock steady, instilling a sense of peaceful surrender — not that her body wasn't already about to explode for want of him.

"Forward a bit more — that's it!" He bent his knees slightly, pressed his cock against her, and drove upward until she was straddling him fully, her legs wrapped around his hips, hugging him into her.

Katya braced herself against the mirror and sink, praying that she wouldn't soil her clothing. Nothing like having a quickie then announcing it to the fellow passengers when she strolled back down the aisle to take her seat.

"Oh!" *Fuck worrying.* She pushed back, thrust for thrust, seeking more of him, near delirium every time he bucked against her. Sweat broke out on her back, and her throat went dry. She'd never been a quiet comer and now she felt the need to scream. She bit back as a yowl of pleasure hammered her. *Oh! Oh! Please...don't stop!*

The familiar giddiness that came from all her blood rushing to one particular body part made her weak. Her eyelids grew heavy, her breath short and quick. Every intimate stroke of his cock inside her pressed her onward towards an impending explosion.

Thunder cracked outside their plane, and Katya jumped, terrified.

Her companion held her closer, almost as if instinctively. "It's just a storm."

"I hate flying." She felt weak, helpless, for more reasons than one. She was in danger to losing touch with reality inside the plane and sure as hell didn't want to face the one outside that door.

"You ready?" His whisper in her ear rubbed like sweet-smelling sandpaper.

"My hormones are having a block party, and you want to know if I'm ready? Put on your sunshades, because the fireworks are about to go off."

Ace nuzzled her throat and suckled the corded muscle on her neck's column. As soon as his tongue stroked her skin, Katya cried out...so loudly that Ace immediately covered her mouth with his hand.

She opened her eyes in surprise, partly in anger. Then she saw the mirth contorting his features as his body pushed towards its own release. They were fucking in a lavatory, for chrissakes, and there she was ready to announce to the other passengers that while they were reading their papers, listening to music, or sleeping, she was riding the hardest cock onboard, legs locked, pussy clenched, demanding satisfaction.

Okay, so I deserved to be silenced. Certainly don't want to get tossed off the plane or remanded to the police once we land. She bucked against him, her pussy's muscles milking Ace's rigid cock for every drop she could get. *Doesn't mean I don't want him just as hot and horny as I am.*

Spasms of pure energy shot through her entire body, and she clung to Ace, greedily wanting more, even though her senses told her she already had more than she could handle. His body shuddering against hers told her that he, too, was completely spent.

What sounded like rain surrounded their cubicle. *Definitely a storm.* Maybe she could get lost in a book or even sleep. *Not likely, but one can hope.*

"There for a second, I wasn't sure which disturbance would be louder." He grinned as he said it.

As her blood flow slowly returned to normal, she became aware of footsteps and muffled voices outside the tiny compartment. Then a knock at the door.

Ace's eyes held hers, and both of them looked like naughty, guilty schoolchildren.

"We've been bad." She kept her voice low and stifled a giggle.

"Very bad." He nodded in agreement as he echoed her sentiments. He unlocked the door and cracked it, peering through the small opening. Then he closed it after giving whoever was on the other side of the door an apologetic smile.

"Remember that chubby lady sitting across the aisle from you? The one with the coat that looked like she had a dead animal for a collar?"

Katya nodded.

"I think she needs to use the lavatory."

The good manners his mother had taught him kicked in. Ace helped Katya right her clothing then tended to his own. When his mystery lady would have opened the door and left, however, he kept one hand on the door to prevent her from opening it and placed the other tenderly on her head, letting his fingers thread through her hair. She lifted bright blue eyes to his and smiled.

He contemplated giving her the jewellery he'd purchased and thought better of it. Somehow, handing her a gift right after they'd had sex seemed inappropriate on so many levels.

He didn't want to cheapen what had happened, even though they'd both been consenting strangers. There was something about her that drew him, made him want to know her, not just her body.

Shit. He was tongue-tied.

She saved him the embarrassment and confusion of being caught with his verbal pants around his knees by standing on tip-toe and giving him a soft kiss on the lips before she opened the door and faced the huffy woman who'd interrupted them.

He waited for her to make her way down the aisle before opening the door and stepping out. Thankfully, no one was around. The flight attendants were busy taking care of refreshments, requests for pillows and blankets, and doing whatever they could to make their passengers comfortable.

Okay, so your gonads are satisfied. He steeled himself not to look at her on his way back to his seat. *But what did you gain by rushing her like that? Whatever happened to asking her name, where she was headed, whether you could call her? Not like you don't already spend half your time on planes. Maybe she lives close enough to your family that you might have a relationship of some sort with her.*

Ace winced. Family. If only it were that easy. He hadn't spoken more than a handful of sentences to any of them since going to Australia. His older brothers had all three been angry for him for dumping the family business onto their shoulders. He knew his old man had expected him to at the very least head the overseas operations, but their estrangement ran deep.

Ever since his mother had died, Randal Elliott had done nothing but badger Ace about his studies, his decisions and his life in general. Randal had disapproved of the college in New York and had threatened to withhold monies to pay for

Ace's education unless his youngest of four went to college in the Midwest. Ace's response, which may have been juvenile at the time, worked. He'd pretty much said a *screw you* to his father and had funded his own education by doing testing assignments for a new game company and by donating sperm at the local sperm bank.

The game company had been a gamble. The company had no assets, little capital, and zilch going for them other than a demand for their products. Ace had grown up with a joystick in one hand and a television remote in the other, so testing new games as they developed had been more of a pleasure than a job. When the then pubescent company had money problems, Ace had cashed in what savings he had and became a partner, taking stock instead of a pay check until Finnegan's Treasure was back in the black.

Now, years later, he and his partners, cousins Mike and Brody Finnegan, were known worldwide, with shops in every corner of the universe, and the generation of players they'd groomed in the nineties now had children of their own who craved their merchandise.

Children. He winced. God help him. After his best friend in Oz had told him of the mothers of all those children seeking him, he'd received a call from David, oldest of Randal's offspring. Dave had been cryptic, as usual, but he'd gotten his point across. It would be in Ace's best interest to fly home and take responsibility for wanking off in a specimen jar. That was what pissed him off the most, that anyone would fault *him*, that *his* privacy might be invaded. Hadn't he provided a service for childless couples? Hadn't he fit the mould they sought, that of a clean-cut, intelligent, not unattractive milkshake daddy?

Fuck the lot of them. He'd go home, talk to his brothers — and to be sure, they all knew about his college excursions if

Dave did. They'd be waiting in ambush for him, most likely at the airport. All Ace was interested in was finding out why now. What purpose did it serve for him to come forward and admit to being anyone's biological father? Not like the parents could sue him for child support—that point had been made abundantly clear when he signed the release papers at the sperm clinic. He, as donor, would be protected and never legally bound by his actions.

Someone, however, at the clinic, had obviously given out his name and information, or Dave wouldn't know about it. Dave, the sensible sibling, was the one brother who would give him grief. Sam, the lone physician in the family, would think it funny and razz him mercilessly. Frank, the accountant brother closest to him in age, would applaud his entrepreneurship. As for their father, Randal would give him the proverbial cold shoulder, think him stupid and irresponsible for not considering the consequences of his actions and consider him a coward for never looking back.

Ace had been on his own for two decades, but it still hurt to know that he was a disappointment to his family, that no matter how much money he amassed, he was a failure in his father's eyes. Never mind that he'd managed to remain single, rich as sin, and head of his own corporation. His older brother thought him a fuck-up, a child who'd never grown up. Dave always lauded family above all else. The man wasn't married but wanted to be—he was just waiting, he said, for the right woman.

What would Mom think? He comforted himself, thinking that Lana would have considered him a success. His mother taught him to prize independent thinking, a clean conscience and a good heart. Lana would have been there for him.

He drummed his fingers on his knees as he thought of his mother. Svetlana Ivanovich had lost her life most likely because of him. The doctors had told her she couldn't have any more children, and her last baby proved difficult for her. She'd named him Alexei after her father, but everyone had called him Alexander or Ace.

When he was born, his maternal grandparents had visited often. After their daughter died, they stopped interacting with the rest of them, almost like it hurt too much to be reminded she was gone.

Ace couldn't remember the last time he'd felt drawn to a maternal figure, so the fact he'd made so many women mothers boggled his brain. He knew one of the reasons he'd donated sperm had been to fund his education, but what nobody else had fathomed was his strongest motivation— that of needing a place to belong, of contributing, of passing along what he hoped where the qualities of a good man or woman…traits he'd inherited from Lana.

He needed to visit the hospital named for her while he was in Kansas City. He hadn't spoken to his Grandfather Ivanovich's best friends, who were on the board, in many years. It was time they caught up.

* * * *

A mile-high fuck with a perfect stranger—and he was indeed perfect in every way visually—was not something Katya had ever considered. Now that she'd done the nasty with him, her conscience pricked her. He didn't know who she was, while she, on the other hand, knew damned near everything except the size of his underwear and what toys were his favourite as a child. A distinct disadvantage to him.

She wished she'd considered the consequences beforehand. Her family would be waiting on her at the airport, and sooner or later he'd see her with his brother and future sister-in-law. Ace Elliott didn't look like the type who believed in coincidence. Ace was a man who determined his own fate.

Idiot. She scolded herself. *You've probably broken all manner of moral and ethical trust.* Her eyes rounded in surprise. Elena hadn't asked her to represent Nik. *Dear God.* If she did, however, that would pose problems, considering Katya had just fucked who would be the defendant, that is if Ace fought to keep his information private. He might take her sexual playfulness as pejoratively as she would have his gratefulness or generosity had he offered her money once they'd pulled up their pants.

What a mess. Katya slipped off the Jimmy Choo platform heels and massaged her feet. Then she dug into the matching leather and suede handbag for the cashmere socks she always carried for long flights.

She frowned. Generosity…

She wondered why Ace had purchased the bracelet she'd admired in the airport shop. She didn't remember hearing he had a girlfriend, much less a spouse, or someone he'd be willing to drop that much money on. But then again, for all she knew, Ace might come from the bourgeoisie that her family in Russia had despised. She'd been too little to recall much about her former homeland, but she'd heard her grandmother speak often enough of the socio-political infrastructures in Russia. Lidia Grishenka's teeth would clench to the point of grinding at just the mention of any ruling social class and the capitalism that distanced them from the rest of the country.

"That is reverse discrimination and snobbery," Katya had kidded her.

"Say that after you've watched *your* sons and daughters struggle to feed their families," the old woman had cracked.

Katya knew better than to argue with her, yet she couldn't help but wonder how Lidia perceived Ace's brother. Surely, Dave was as much the *born-with-a-silver-spoon-in-his-mouth* type as Ace.

She shook her head. Nonsense. To even contemplate what Lidia would think of a man she'd just screwed was ludicrous. Lidia would never have the opportunity to even meet Ace, much less make judgment calls about him.

Katya's father, Maxim, Lidia's youngest son, was far more tolerant than his mother. Maxim understood the American idealist thinking that had made many immigrants comfortable if not wealthy. *Learn the language, learn the thought processes, and you'll get ahead.*

If only Lidia could set aside her inbred bigotry and distrust for the wealthy. Katya was weary of toning down her wardrobe every time she went home for a visit. It felt like dumbing down to a man who couldn't handle the fact that her IQ was off the charts.

For love of her grandmother, though, she pretended she wasn't doing as well as she was as an attorney. She suffered the looks from Lidia that clearly said *poor child, can't find a man*, as well.

Only her father totally understood. Her mother was more inclined towards Lidia's thinking — Anisa wanted grandchildren and didn't understand why Katya would rather have a career. Katya's brother and sisters were more vested in their own emotional growth and personal relationships and didn't think much about money at all.

I must be a throwback to the eighties yuppies. Katya smiled to herself. She'd stop at the airport bathrooms and change into the track suit she'd stuffed into her carry-on bag at the last minute before leaving Sydney. That would at least keep Lidia from pursing her lips and asking how much the heels cost.

She snuggled into her seat and relaxed. Her accommodations were nothing special, but they'd have to do, and her quivering muscles told her to take a much-needed nap.

Turbulence rocked the aircraft, and Katya bit back a scream as she and the other passengers pitched slightly. She closed her eyes and fought the panic that climbed from her solar plexus to her throat. When she was able to focus, she glanced at her watch. She'd apparently slept for several hours.

The intercom kicked on and the pilot's voice spoke soothingly to them, but Katya heard the concern in his voice. "We're diverting to Hawaii within the hour. Reports are that the storm headed for Malaysia has turned. It'll be chasing us into Hilo International Airport, but we should land and have you on your way to the hotels before the worst of the weather hits."

Katya blinked. *Storm – chasing us?* She resisted the urge to leave her seat and fly towards the first class passengers where she knew Ace would be. He was a stranger, but somehow the thought of his arms about her during an ordeal such as this comforted her. *Hotels? We're staying overnight?*

Why hadn't she gotten his telephone number? She'd bet Ace was equipped with one of those expensive cell phones that did everything but cook breakfast.

Another bumpy patch of air. Katya bit her bottom lip so hard she tasted blood. She looked about and saw other worried passengers, people whose eyes were filled with terror. This was so not how she'd envisioned her evening, strapped into a bucket seat, miles above the ground, with a storm repeatedly chewing them and spitting them back out.

She tried concentrating on her family and friends, and when that didn't work she switched gears and conjured images of her work, various clients, courthouses where she'd tried cases—anything but what was going on outside the hollowed-out bullet called a plane that was headed for what seemed certain disaster.

What seemed like hours ticked by, and although cabin pressure remained stabilised, she fully expected the oxygen masks to drop and for people to scramble for their last breaths.

But the plane didn't hurtle—it glided downward, roughly yet firmly on course, apparently, because the 'oh shit' sign she half-expected didn't appear and the lights on the ground rose to meet them steadily, instilling a calming effect.

Christ, Katya. You're alive. She buried her face in her hands and focused on her breathing. *Not like you can help anyone else who might need it if you don't check your own pulse first.*

When she looked up, her fellow travellers were unbuckling their seatbelts and reaching for their luggage in the overhead compartments. Katya willed herself to remain seated until the crowd in the aisles had thinned.

And there he was, hand outstretched, looking as calm as if he'd just had drinks at the top of the world and wanted to see what all the fuss was about. His fingers beckoned her to accept his assistance.

She touched his hand, and as if by magic, her fears melted, as did the energy supporting her legs. He tugged her out of her seat, into the aisle. She collapsed against him and felt his arms go around her. Then all her thoughts imploded, and she mumbled something, hugging the biceps and forearms cradling her…until she could no longer feel anything.

Chapter Two

Ace had a moment of fear when he felt the weight of her body fall against him. He wasn't afraid of dropping her, but he was worried she may have some medical condition that wasn't apparent. What if she was diabetic and the trauma of their air adventure had sent her glucose level spiralling? What if she was anaemic?

When she mumbled, "God I hate flying," he bit back a smile and breathed easier. She was a bit shell-shocked. *That's all*, he told himself.

The emergency landing had been unnerving, but Ace had flown so often that such things as bad weather rarely gave him reason to pause. If anything, this might be fortuitous if she was agreeable to what he had planned.

"Sit up if you can." He touched her face with the damp paper towel the stewardess had provided. "We've landed."

His recent paramour blinked against the light as her eyes focused. "We're...okay?"

"Outside of a torrential rain and cyclone winds, we're fine." He thumbed over his shoulder. "There are a few people who'd like to find shelter before the eye of the storm hits, though. Think you can stand?"

She nodded, a sheepish, apologetic smile creasing her pale features. "I am *so* sorry. I don't usually pass out."

"Yeah?" Ace snapped his fingers and lowered his voice to a conspiratorial whisper. "And here I was hoping to sweep you off of your feet tonight and make love to you until you did just that."

Then she seemed to recall their passionate encounter in the lavatory and sat upright so fast that Ace wasn't surprised to see her a bit dizzy.

He brushed the back of his fingers against her cheek. "Come on. We have a taxi waiting on us."

The airline officials were quick to check baggage and send all their passengers to the hotel nearest the airport, but Ace intervened and requested his and his companion's luggage be sent to a new bed and breakfast west of town.

"If that's all right with you?" He posed his words as both statement and question.

"A bed and a bath? How can I refuse such an offer?" The blonde grinned weakly.

Ace responded in kind. "I'm hoping to make it impossible."

He tried not to make a big deal out of collecting her bags, but he took a couple of extra seconds to study the signature on the nametags. *Katya Grishenka*. Ah, a Russian bombshell. What the hell was she doing in Australia?

Ace chided himself. What did it matter? Wasn't he a foreigner who'd been working in Sydney? Perhaps her family lived in Oz.

"The name's Ace, by the way, and I promise I'm not some pervert—you don't need to be afraid of me." His eyes narrowed as he studied her.

"Well, damn. You're no fun."

She gave him an open-mouthed smile that made his cock flame. Ace considered for a second that maybe it was he who should be afraid once they were alone.

"Do you have--?" Her voice held concern.

"Our itineraries? Re-boarding information?" He patted his jacket pocket. "Right here. Our new flight leaves at ten tomorrow morning. It appears our plane is getting a check-out." He hastened to add, "Nothing wrong with it. One of those maintenance things they do when the weather is rotten."

Ace smiled when she seemed to accept what he said.

"And this place where we're spending the night?"

He hugged her briefly. "Nice. Really nice, according to my secretary."

Katya frowned and stood back. "You've spoken to someone in your office?"

"Well, we're stranded for a few hours," he said. "So I called corporate headquarters and had someone find accommodations that fit our needs." Then he grinned broadly. "In answer to that question in your eyes, you were only out a few minutes. I'd made the call from the plane's phone once the pilot said we were landing in Hilo."

There were small eateries within the terminal, and according to Meg at Elliott Enterprises, there were several places still open on route to their bed and breakfast.

He caught himself fantasising about Katya. Maybe this change of plans was fortuitous and the beginning of a nice friendship with her.

"Jesus." Katya sounded relieved. "Food. I'm starving."

"Then let's get moving so we can find you something to nibble."

She wasn't touching that remark with a ten-foot pole, even if Ace had one. The raging storm, the idea that they might have crash-landed sent chills zipping along her spine. On the other hand, knowing she'd have a few hours more with Ace was deliciously appealing.

After a few moments of silence and quiet looks, Ace held one of her hands in his. The young man driving the cab kept looking into his rear-view mirror, his small, dark eyes showing curious concern.

Their cabbie was a talkative Japanese man named Daisuke. He pointed to the kanji spelling proudly. "It mean 'great help'." He thumped his chest. "I can show you anything you want to see on Hilo. My ancestors live here since early last century."

Katya glanced at Ace's face. He seemed intrigued but reluctant to take a tour. "Maybe when it's not raining so hard."

"How about restaurants? We got seafood, steaks, and desserts. Liliko'i Cheesecake quite interesting.

Katya couldn't help but butt in. "What's that?"

Daisuke grinned. "New York cheesecake with mac nut crust and fruit topping. Specialty around here, can't get in New York. You want me to take you? They still open."

"Sure." Ace was quick to comply. He rested his hand on Katya's knee, making her jump. "We can take the food back to the hotel. No?"

She nodded. "Steaks? Shrimp? Anything with meat and veggies?"

He made her jump again. "Anything you want. Tonight is yours."

Katya stayed in the cab, listening to Daisuke's horror stories of past tsunamis while Ace shopped. She didn't want to be rude, because the tales were fascinating, but they were also scaring the shit out of her, considering why her plane had landed in the first place that night.

When Ace returned, the automobile filled with delicious smells of what he told her were Asian-inspired pizzas and calzones, along with side dishes. "I couldn't help myself." He chuckled. "Must be the weather, or an incentive to build up my strength for the night."

"Don't get your hopes up," she replied. "I'm hungrier than I am horny right now."

"So I'll feed you first and feel you up later."

Katya's first instinct upon seeing their bedroom was to fall onto the mattress, but common sense rooted her to the doorway entrance. "I need to phone my sister and tell her where I am."

Ace waved towards the phone. "I have my cell if you don't wish to place the call from there."

"I have a cell, but thanks." She shimmied out of her coat and allowed him to hang it up for her. "I'm just wondering what time it is there."

Ace turned while opening the closet door. "We're two hours ahead of Los Angeles, if that helps."

Katya thought a second. "Thanks. So we're four hours ahead of the Midwest."

She closed her eyes briefly, cursing herself. She hadn't meant to reveal so much just yet.

"So we're on the same flight from LA into…?"

"Kansas for me." Guilt engulfed her. The air she breathed felt constricted as she spoke. She sat on the bed and tugged at her shoes, setting them aside. "There's something I need to tell you."

He shook his head. "No. Not that I want secrets between us, I'd just like to have this one night of complete abandonment, with no worries for either of us." He laughed.

"So unless you have some dreadful disease, can it wait until morning?"

Katya felt a gentle pull on her heartstrings. He was so damned trusting, and here she was setting him up, knowing full well what awaited him when he stepped off of the plane in Kansas City.

"I take it by your silence that there's something wrong?"

When she looked up, his hands were on his hips and mild concern creased his brow.

He seemed weary. Despite his take-charge behaviour at the airport and his general quiet, John Wayne demeanour, his eyes spoke volumes. No telling what sort of business or personal dealings he faced when they landed. Katya's maternal instincts kicked into high gear. She wanted to smooth his brow, stroke his hair, massage his shoulders and tell him everything would work out. But she couldn't in good conscience say such a thing, knowing Nik's situation and Ace's potential involvement.

"No, I'm fine. No diseases, no husband waiting to clobber both of us, no major malfunctions in my personal life."

Relief etched his face. "Good. Then maybe for one brief moment in time we can just enjoy one another's company, have a nice meal and see what follows."

She warred with herself. Stranded over night with sexy Ace Elliott—she'd be a fool not to jump at the chance for a few more hours in his arms.

"So let's eat when I get back—the food will keep. I'll go down to the desk and check the weather reports while you're busy." Ace pulled on the jacket he had begun to remove.

"That's not necessary." A sense of alarm made her twinge. She didn't want him to feel ousted in his own quarters.

Ace seemed nonplussed. "You're entitled to your privacy, and I'll only be downstairs. Sure, I could turn on the television up here, but it's much more interesting to get a local's take on our situation. I'll be back shortly." He crossed the room once more to drop a kiss on her upturned face.

Katya felt strange, wanting him to stay, needing him to leave while she made the call. *If only I'd come clean with him the moment we met.*

* * * *

Had he made a mistake in taking her to a private location away from the others? What if she'd wanted her own room?

Ace spied the woman who'd checked them in and sauntered up to her. She looked to be about sixty, a mixture of Japanese and Polynesian, and she reminded him of the stout actress who'd sang "Bali Ha'i" in the film "South Pacific". A much shorter, smaller woman was with her.

"I came to ask about the weather." He hoped the statement would spark their interest. It did, only not the way he expected.

"Why would you leave that pretty young thing upstairs all by herself to come down here and talk about something as inconsequential as the weather?" The short woman frowned, but it was obvious she was ribbing him.

"She had important phone calls to make." He winked.

"Ha." The larger woman put in her two cents. "She probably just told you that to see if you'd stick around."

"Hey, I know when I'm not wanted or needed." Ace tried to be nonchalant.

The two older women weren't having any of it. One took his arm and led him to a small boutique area, pointing out what she considered perfect gifts for a lady friend. "Maybe a gift will keep her thoughts away from the telephone. Nothing too personal." Her fingers trailed a bright, flowered sarong then flitted to a shell necklace. "On the other hand, jewellery speaks volumes, and this is hardly ostentatious."

Ace purchased both items. "You sure you're not a car salesman in disguise?"

While the ladies wrapped his gifts, he strolled out to the covered veranda and watched sheets of rain pelting the earth just beyond the house. *I really should phone Dave and tell him I'll be late. Doubtful he'll even be at the airport, though.* Men in his acquaintance weren't as high maintenance as women when it came to things like goodbyes and arrivals.

He chuckled as he thought of the first gift he'd purchased for Katya, back in Sydney. "Dumbass, you haven't given her the first box." He'd never been one for gift-buying—his own secretary was lucky she didn't have to shop for herself. What had come over him?

Screw it. He reached into his jacket pocket for his cell phone. Might as well at least be courteous and let Dave know he'd be late.

The phone didn't ring but a couple of times. Then Dave answered without even saying hello. "Where are you?"

Ace snorted. "It's good to hear your voice, too. I'm in Hawaii, Hilo to be precise."

"What the hell are you doing there? You're supposed to be in Los Angeles within the hour."

Perturbed, Ace walked to the back of the gift shop so that the two ladies couldn't hear him. "What bug crawled up your ass and died?"

His sibling's tone was sombre, his voice deep and low. "Ace, I don't know where to begin."

Dave alarmed him. Sure, he was the most serious of all his brothers, and, yes, he was the bossiest, but he wasn't an alarmist. A knot formed in Ace's stomach. "Spill it."

"Have you met Katya yet?"

For a moment, Ace thought he'd misunderstood. How could his brother in Kansas possibly know her? "We've met." His facial muscles clenched despite his resolve to remain calm. *Met? Well, can't exactly say I've fucked her without stirring up a shit storm if she's important to him.*

"And?"

"Just tell me, Dave…and what?" Now he was impatient.

"Ace, there are people here who wish to speak with you when you arrive."

Ace rolled his eyes and groaned, stifling the urge to lambaste his brother. "Well, tell them to take a number and shove it up their asses. I have meetings scheduled from tomorrow through next Friday." Ace consciously lowered his voice when he looked up and saw the two older women staring at him. "What does that have to do with Katya?"

"She hasn't told you?"

"Apparently not. For Christ's sake, what are you trying to say? What is it I'm supposed to know that I obviously don't?"

"Fuck, Ace. It's about the kids."

The knot in his stomach twisted tightly. Ace closed his eyes as his head began throbbing. "The kids." It was a statement, not a question. He was busted. Dave knew, and so did Katya. What sort of sick game had she been playing with him? Who was she to these kids?

Just the thought of the word made him ill. He opened his eyes and looked for the nearest trash basket, just in case he upchucked. The pain in his stomach and head were severe enough to warrant worry. There was nowhere to sit, and the only thing to lean against was a display case containing jewellery.

Jewellery. He felt even sicker. He'd purchased a thousand dollar bracelet for the tramp, not to mention a sarong and a necklace. She had to know her effect on him. He'd practically handed her his balls and told her to beat him to death with them.

Another thought crashed his consciousness. Katya was an attorney. Fucking hell, did she represent one of those kids? All of them? Who was she?

Whatever his brother had been saying was lost on him. "I'm sorry, Dave, could you repeat that?"

"Are you alright?" Dave sounded worried.

"Oh, thank you for asking. It's nothing—just a major malfunction in my brain, because I could have sworn you just told me that the woman I fucked on the plane is doing some covert operation that involves orphans looking for their sperm donor."

"You fucked her? Christ, Ace!"

"Well, it wasn't exactly first on my list to ask her if she happened to represent any biological children I might have, Dave! Not like it's a pickup line, up there with *What's your sign*, is it?"

Dave swore softly. "Damn it, Ace, I'm asking if you're okay because I care."

"I'll be fine. Just tell me what this is all about, and don't say the kids again—that much I've figured out. What specifically do they want from me?"

"They don't want anything!"

"Then why are we having this conversation, Dave?"

Dave's tone changed from concerned to contrite. "I'm sorry—Katya should have told you this by now. Her sister sent her a photo of you so she'd recognise you."

"Goddamnit, does everybody know how I earned money in college?" Ace's voice rose again, and this time he didn't give a shit if the two women across the room heard him or not. "What the fuck does her sister have to do with this?"

"I'd appreciate it if you'd lower your voice, Ace, and I'm sure whoever is within earshot there would as well. Her sister is my fiancé, and the little boy who needs your help is her son."

Ace laughed nervously—he couldn't help himself. "Your fiancé? And one of my sperm made it all the way from New York to Kansas?"

"You're being an ass."

"No, you're being an ass. I call to tell you I'll be a day or two late, and you hit me with this shit? All of you were in on this and were just willing to let me waltz into the Kansas City airport and get nabbed by who? The cops? Feds? Sperm Gestapo?"

"Just calm down!"

"Get fucked. I'm outta here, and this time, don't bother trying to locate me. I'll get buried so far in the Australian bush that even Crocodile Dundee couldn't find me."

"Ace, you can't do that! He's your son, and he needs help!"

A protest the size of God's balls formed in Ace's mind, but he couldn't utter a sound for fear he'd squeak. He had an arsenal of sarcasm and denial aimed and ready to fire, but his throat tightened to the point that he had to concentrate just to push air through it.

My son. The words brought tears to his eyes. Not a specimen in a plastic cup, not a gleam in a potential parent's eyes, but a live human being with his DNA.

"Ace?"

"You said he needs help." Ace struggled to keep his voice steady. "He's in trouble?"

"He's sick, Ace. He needs a bone marrow transplant."

Choking with emotion, Ace could barely breathe, much less speak. He tried twice and couldn't. Finally, he mumbled, "I'll call you back."

Emotions he'd never felt made every nerve in his body tingle with fear, dread, anticipation, excitement, and self-loathing. One child, among how many? Would he experience the same mixture of pleasure and pain every time he heard about one of them? What they expected of him was no longer an issue — he was suddenly faced with what he expected of himself.

Do the right thing. That's what his father would have told him. Whatever the hell that was. *Search your heart,* his mother would have said.

Fuck me and I'll lead you around by the nose until I get you where I want you is what he imagined coming from Katya's sexy lips.

The thought of the blonde angered him beyond belief. What was he, some ABF, asshole biological father, to be used like a whore just because he'd ejaculated for money in his teens and early twenties?

The karmic wheel of life spun quickly and bit him square on the ass. *Time for a reckoning if not redemption.*

What he wanted to do was jump on the next plane bound for Sydney and do as he'd sworn to Dave, make it that far then travel north and simply disappear for a few years. *Find my ass in north Victoria singing "Waltzing Matilda", or better yet, see if you can find me in the damn outback of Queensland.* Ace took a shuddering breath and blew the air out in quick, short bursts, concentrating on regulating his pulse.

He felt his lips curve into an evil smile as he thought of Katya. Maybe she was only doing what her sister and his brother had asked her to do…bring him home. He'd thought she was as attracted to him as he was to her, but now he'd never know. He could sure make her uncomfortable as hell until they reached Kansas, though.

He sobered considerably when he realised how quickly his thoughts had turned. He would continue on the journey, go to the Midwest, see what he could do to help Dave's son-to-be.

My son.

* * * *

Katya's conversation with Elena was filled with dread. Nik was in remission, but the doctors were anxious about whether or not they'd find a suitable donor in time before fever once again ravaged the child's body, before his vital signs all began showing alarming precursors to trouble.

What the doctors needed right now was a blood test from Ace. From there, the two tablespoons or however much they used was tested for six out of the four antigens unique to each person, and this test alone took about three weeks. Time was precious. A second battery of tests lasting nearly a month would be held, and then if Ace was a match, he'd have to undergo surgery to have marrow from his hip extracted.

It was up to Katya to convince Ace to trust her, to have the first test as soon as possible. *This is no game – I'm in too deep. I have to ask him when he gets back.*

She felt guilty, not because of what Ace would endure – donors spent a minimal amount of time in hospital after surgery, as little as one day. She felt bad for having deceived him thus far, for becoming involved with him. He was certainly attractive, but there was a vulnerability, a subtle sweetness that appealed to her. He may have spent his entire adulthood as a bachelor, and he may have not given a second thought to whether or not he had children. As head of his own corporation, he was most likely a tad ruthless and even detached, not becoming emotionally connected during business meetings.

This was different, though. She hoped with all her heart that he would acquiesce, that he'd not only go willingly but with a spirited hope. Nik needed him—they all needed him—to be supportive, not resentful and dragging his heels.

Katya cradled the phone, nerves jittery. She was about to take a shower when she heard Ace's key card in the lock.

She could tell by his face that something wasn't right. "How's the weather looking?"

"Stormy." His eyes were a flat, smoky black. He looked like he'd just eaten a bad meal.

"You know." Her heart sank.

Ace nodded. "When did you plan on telling me? Was this to be item number two on your list of things to share about yourself?"

Katya rushed towards him. "I didn't know I was going to feel this way about you."

"What way?" His voice was angry.

"That we'd...make love."

He closed the door behind him and leaned against it. "I wouldn't call that making love—that was fucking, and you knew when we did it what I'd be up against once we landed in Kansas."

She nodded, ashamed, and tears welled in her eyes.

"Oh, no!" he exclaimed. "Don't cry. You've used every other trick, but not that, please."

Katya swelled with indignation. "I'm not crying for you! I'm crying for me, because I care, and for Nikanor, who needs you." She swiped at the tear already cascading down her cheeks. "Whatever you think of me, put it aside, for him."

"Just tell me one thing. When did you know?"

"Weeks ago. I saw you at a party at Travis's house, but I ducked out. I was afraid to meet you."

"You, afraid?" He snorted.

"Yes! You were attractive, and you seemed so nice. I couldn't afford to become involved with you—I had a job to do."

"Now I'm a project."

"You are Nik's only hope…"

Ace raised his hands, palms out as if warding off some evil spirit. "Save your breath. I'm still going to Kansas, and I'll take the blasted blood test. If I'm a good candidate, I'll even donate, because that's the kind of guy I am—I'd have done this for any child. Just don't try convincing me that what we had meant anything to you."

He looked past her at their meal. His face reflected sadness, grief, anger, and confusion. "Small world, isn't it? I mean, that I helped give birth to someone who wound up living in my own home state. What are the odds?"

"His mother was from New York."

Ace shook his head. "I don't want to know about her. Not yet. I'm still digesting that I have a child, a son, that I'm about to meet."

Katya's conscience warred with her common sense. Should she tell him? She took a deep breath and forged ahead. "Nik has a twin sister, Nina—she'll be there when we arrive."

He looked like she'd slapped him. "Ah." He blinked. "Any more there?"

Katya gave a nervous laugh. "No. Just the two."

"How old are they?"

For someone who didn't want to know anything, he appeared to be at least curious.

"Six."

Ace frowned. "Then they're not mine. I haven't been to the sperm bank for well over a decade."

Katya repressed a smile. "My niece and nephew were in the frozen foods section of the supermarket."

The furrow between his brows deepened. "Pardon me?"

"Sperm is often frozen," Katya explained. "The twins' mother obviously picked up a deposit that had been kept on ice."

"Ha!" He immediately brushed a hand over his mouth after the rapid outburst. "Sorry. What else can you tell me about them?"

Oh screw the consequences. "They both look like you—your eyes." She touched her temples. "That streak in their hair."

"Really?" He leaned forward and pushed himself off of the door. He shrugged. "I'm at a loss here. I really don't know what to say."

"I really wish you'd let me tell you how they came to us."

Ace sighed. "Fuck it. Go ahead, but I need a drink while we're having this discussion. I've had about all the news— good and bad—that I can handle without reinforcements."

Katya sat on the edge of the bed while he rummaged through the small liquor cabinet in their room. When he asked if she'd like a drink, she gladly said yes. No telling how long the storm outside would rage, and she wanted to quell any thought of one erupting inside. Maybe if she was under the influence she would feel at least a little numb and not so frightened.

He poured the drinks then sat next to her on the bed, kicking his shoes off then placing them near the closet. "I don't suppose you have a photo of them?" He lifted his glass in salute and drained it with one large gulp.

Katya didn't expect his interest in her nephew and niece. She nodded wordlessly, eager to have something to do besides feel like shit. "Their first school photos—they're in my purse."

She took her time, searching to see if she had any more photos to show him. "I apologise for taking so long. I thought perhaps I had a shot of them last summer when Elena first..."

She turned to show him the pictures in her hand and found him flat on his back, eyes closed, snoring peacefully.

The storm raged about them, causing the electricity to flicker. She set the photos on the bedside table and took the empty glass from his hand to place near the photos. Then she lay down beside him, snuggling against him tentatively, careful not to awaken him.

Let him sleep. He's had a long day, the first in a week of what may very well drain him of whatever desires he's held onto regarding having a family of his own.

She placed a hand against his chest, feeling the soft rise and fall. The fabric was soft, buttery, sensual. Hardly *daddy* material. Not that she had anything to go on but her own father, whose broadcloth button downs that he wore to work were all she had as a daddy shirt reference.

Katya inhaled slowly, deeply, still wondering how to deal with Ace. How did daddies smell? Her own smelled of soap and musk. Ace, however had a scent of his own that she couldn't identify, a blend of subtle, expensive men's cologne.

She looked at what skin his shirt revealed. He had the kind of tan that made women nervous and men jealous. It was crazy to even contemplate the thought of Ace befriending Nik and Nina, much less becoming Uncle Ace, a daddy in his own right some day. He was too much the jet-setter, the nomad, the loose canon.

Katya sighed and choked back tears. She felt it safe to assume Ace had a special kind of mental hell when he thought about the possibilities of all the children he may have fathered, which was a shame. She knew firsthand how terrific at least two of those kids were.

She barely knew Ace, yet it saddened her to think that he might never feel those tiny arms about his neck and some child whispering *I love you, Daddy* in his ear, that he'd never know the value or the joy he'd given to others.

He stirred beneath her touch, startling her. "Katya?"

She held her breath a moment before answering. "Yes?"

"Why are you crying?" He raised his head slightly and stared into her eyes.

She swallowed hard. "It's stupid." She brushed aside his hand when he attempted to lift her chin. "Forget it."

Ace sat up in bed. "I feel a cigarette coming on — in fact, half a pack." He searched for the pack and lighter. "Spill it, Katya. We have enough secrets, don't you think?"

"You want the truth? I cry for you. I feel sorry for you, that you will never know what it feels like to have your child's arms about your neck and hear them telling you that they love you."

He looked like she'd slapped him. "Really?" He lit two cigarettes and handed her one then placed the ashtray between them. "Care to explain?"

"This has nothing to do with my nephew and niece."

"Right." Sarcasm dripped from his words. "You're not being judgmental at all, huh?"

"Actually, no. I just think it's a shame you close yourself off the way you do."

"You've known me a few hours, and you feel qualified to say that to me?" His voice was incredulous.

"I do." She lifted her chin and stared at him. "When things get personal, you withdraw."

Ace exploded. "Well, goddamn, I wonder why?" He took a deep drag and let the smoke out in a rush. "I have a secret—

people do, you know? And my secret is something I didn't expect to come back and bite me in the ass years down the road. I did what I did to put myself through college. I had no intentions of hurting anyone."

"I'm not talking about that! What you did as a teenager and whatever you do regarding Nik has nothing to do with this conversation!"

"Doesn't it? You expect me to do the right thing, don't you?"

"Hope, Ace. But, yes, after knowing you, even for a few hours, I expect it, too. Because that's who you really are—you just hide behind this façade. You act like you don't give a damn about anyone, but you do. You should have seen your face when I told you that you have a son and a daughter, not two kids you'll never see, but two babies who are a part of you."

His face softened, his eyes wide with a sweet concern that tore at her heart. She snapped her fingers. "That look. The one that is curious, interested, worried, and full of wonder. You want to meet them."

"Well, looks like I don't really have much choice."

"See? You have a smartass comeback, you try sarcasm to avoid intimacy, and that's okay." She flung her free hand wildly. "I don't care. Get angry."

He snuffed out his cigarette. "If you're hoping I'll lose my temper, hit you or do something outrageous, you'll have a long wait. That's not my style."

Katya grabbed the ashtray and ripped her cigarette's cherry viciously across the glass. "Whatever, Ace. Have your pity party—but have it without me."

She leapt off of the bed.

"Where are you going?"

"I'd rather sleep in the goddamn lobby than with you."

"Yeah?" He reached for her hands and pulled her back onto the bed. "That's not what you were saying earlier."

"Earlier, you weren't an asshole."

"Sure I was, and you didn't give a damn. You knew all about me before you even fucked me in the airplane."

Katya smacked her palms against his chest. "Will you get over yourself? Being a sperm donor doesn't make you an asshole. Asshole!"

Ace laughed, and soon she quit fighting and sat beside him again, laughing, too.

"So what constitutes an asshole these days?" Ace asked.

"Convoluting the truth, looking for loopholes to keep from dealing with what's on the table."

"I suppose." He hugged her and lay back down, pulling her with him. "So. What is on the table?"

"I never intended to like you this much."

He nodded. "Fair enough. If I'd known who you were, I wouldn't have fucked you."

"Yes, you would have."

He acquiesced quickly. "Okay, you have me there."

Katya punched him in the gut, making him double forward. "You're so easy, except when it comes to communication."

He groaned. "I'm sorry. We'll talk about whatever you want, just don't assume anything."

She eyed him suspiciously. "Such as?"

"That I'd do the right thing."

"Fine."

"Don't suppose that I won't either. I don't like being played."

"Ah. I see. You'd like to keep some semblance of being in control?" She nodded. "Great. Can we fuck, already?"

Ace grinned. "Now who's easy?"

He peeled her clothing slowly from her body, growling his pleasure as he nibbled her curves and gently nipped her skin, licking a blazing trail of heat from her navel to the juncture of her thighs. "You smell delicious."

Katya resisted running her fingers through his hair. Instead, she gripped the headboard, flexing, twisting, and moaning while she savoured his touch. Why in hell was she attracted to *bad boys*, she wondered. Why couldn't she fall for a true nerd, someone less experienced with women's bodies, less sure of himself?

His tongue speared her moist centre, and her fingers curled tightly. God, he was good! She cried his name softly, eliciting a chuckle from him when he rose momentarily to remove his clothes.

"If that's your only hope of making me think you still think I'm an asshole…"

She laughed and leaned forward, beckoning him back onto the bed then sliding her hands beneath his armpits until she could anchor herself. Digging in her heels on the bed, she pulled Ace forward, on top of her. "Just fuck me, fool. How much cheerleading do you need before you know I want you?"

Ace slid expertly between her legs and finger fucked her, watching her eyes. "This meet with your approval?"

"No!"

He insinuated himself further, teasing her pussy with his cock. "How about that?"

"You're learning."

Ace's grin widened. "One thing I totally adore about you, Katya, is your inability to hide your true feelings."

"Does that mean you trust me?"

"No. It means that I trust myself when I'm with you." His face darkened. "Which for some odd reason is more reassuring than anything I've felt in a long, long time."

He pushed, entering her, and when she'd have turned her head, he called her back. "Please. I'm asking you to trust me now. Look at me. I want to see your eyes as we make love this time."

Katya shivered. Love? Did he realise how much she needed to know that he wasn't just fucking her, despite her flip manner of instigating their copulation?

She nodded slowly and kissed him. Ace responded by deepening their union. His lips were soft yet firm, teasing yet insistent. Katya gave herself to him without reservation. If all she was to have was this, she'd take it.

What Ace didn't realise was that she was no longer playing him—he was playing her, with not only her permission, but her assistance, and if she got her heart broken, it was worth it.

"This time tomorrow…" Ace started to say.

Katya placed a finger against his lips. "We'll be in Kansas." She snuggled against him. "We have a few hours to enjoy one another's company tonight then several hours on another airplane. But let's not think about it? Let's concentrate on this moment. Tomorrow will take care of itself."

Ace nodded and seemed grateful. He renewed their lovemaking with a fervour that frightened her, as if he, too, was reluctant to leave her arms and what they'd shared.

Katya clung to him, her pussy tightening around his cock, her arms locked about his shoulders. She inhaled his essence, savouring the moment and unwilling to let it go.

Chapter Three

He could hardly walk out of the airplane shit-faced, but that's exactly what Ace wanted to do. He studied the ground below as the plane circled then levelled out above the landing strip in Kansas. Clouds separated, revealing velvety green and brown strips of land below, turning the ground into a patchwork quilt of various textures and colours.

How is it that you understand mechanical engineering, physics, graphic design and the million and one other things that comprise devising, implementing and marketing video games, but you don't know Jack Schitt about women? Ace gave himself a mental thrashing as he rose from his seat once the plane landed.

He cleared his luggage out of the overhead compartment then sat back down. Waiting for Katya would be the gentlemanly thing to do. It would also make things easier on his and her family for the two of them to be seen together, united for Nik. The lot of them probably expected the worst of him, considering all of this had just been sprung on him on the way from Australia to the States. He wouldn't give his own family the satisfaction of thinking he was off his guard, and he certainly didn't want to give her relations cause to doubt his sanity and temperament.

When she passed forward, he touched her arm to get her attention. "I thought we'd walk out together." He reached for the larger of the two bags Katya held and grasped the handle.

She seemed confused but pleased. "All right." She waited for him to rise and follow her.

Ace spotted Dave before he noticed the others. His brother, like all of the Elliott men, was tall and lanky, with the same dark hair and eyes. Hands and arms full with briefcase, coat and Katya's tote, he lifted his chin in salute. Dave seemed relieved.

"I was afraid you'd storm off of the plane like a scalded cat." Dave grabbed him and gave him a bear hug.

"And give your fiancée fodder for a fight? Not a chance." Ace stood back and looked at the woman beside Dave. "You must be Elena?"

She nodded and tiptoed to kiss his cheek. "Thank you for coming." Her voice was choked with emotion—a mixture of grief, sadness, and fear, if her eyes reflected what she felt.

Ace swallowed a lump in his throat. He wasn't even sure how he felt, so he figured it best to merely acknowledge her gratitude. He turned back to Dave. "Let's do it."

Dave seemed to know precisely what he meant. "Katya's parents are at the hospital with Nik—you can meet them there."

It was then that Ace noticed the slender child holding Katya's free hand. She looked to be about six and had the saddest, most arresting dark eyes he'd ever seen on a child. A streak of frosty blonde mingled with the rest of her hair, which was a soft brown, and he knew immediately who she was. Nina, Nik's twin. A lump formed in his throat, and he could scarcely breath. This was his daughter.

She tugged on Katya's hand and whispered. "Baba Lidia stayed home. She said somebody had to cook the Thanksgiving dinner."

Ace wanted to hear her speak again, but Dave pulled him towards the baggage claim area. *Baba*, he knew, was an endearment meaning grandmother.

His eyes met Katya's above the child's head. Katya smiled sadly, and he wondered what she was thinking. Did she imagine he'd retreat into his own thoughts now that they were among others? Was he really as self-absorbed as she'd made him out to be? What had she said? That he convoluted the truth, basically that he avoided intimacy by using sarcasm. He'd have to watch what he said. He might be the asshole she'd accused him of being, but he'd never considered that he was less than honest, even with himself.

He couldn't help but snort at the word *Thanksgiving*. He'd spent so many holidays in motels, on airplanes and in foreign countries that the word held little personal meaning for him anymore. It was ironic, he thought, that the word conjured up vague references to hotel restaurants rather than family sit-down dinners, and here he was about to experience his first home-cooked Thanksgiving meal in ages with a group of first-generation Americans. There was an odd symmetry to the idea.

* * * *

Katya wasn't surprised when Ace decided to check into a hotel rather than go home with his brother or spend the night at her parents' home. They both left their luggage in Dave's car for the time being.

They'd all gone to the hospital, and while everyone else went to Nik's room, she went with Ace to get his blood work done. He seemed to already know the hospital, which surprised her.

"Now that we're here and you've agreed to the blood test, I wish you'd reconsider. Something doesn't feel right." She kept pace with him as they walked past the main lobby for the elevators.

"What's wrong?" He paused mid-stride.

"Why are you going through with this?" Her eyes shimmered with unshed tears.

Ace quirked an eyebrow. "Well, it's not out of some misplaced sense of obligation to the kids or because I want to get in your pants, so relax."

"Have you been here before?"

He glanced at her as he pressed the elevator button. "Why do you ask?"

"Why don't you answer?" *Why is he so damned afraid of letting anyone know him, know what he's thinking?* His curt response irritated her.

When the doors opened, Ace pressed the correct button without responding until the doors shut. Then he pointed to a metal sign above the doors. *Svetlana Ivanovich Memorial Children's Hospital.* "Want to know where I got the silver streak in my hair? The one my offspring seem to have inherited? She gave it to me."

Katya leaned against the nearest elevator wall and sighed. "You're talking in riddles."

"My whole life is one big riddle."

The elevator stopped, and they stepped into a quiet corridor. Ace directed her towards the nurses' station. A matronly black woman dressed in hospital scrubs smiled broadly and stuck out her hand for him to shake.

"Mr. Elliott, what a nice surprise! Are you here to see Dr. Ward?"

"Hello, Beverly. No, I'm here for some lab work if anyone's available."

She frowned but nodded. "Sure. Give me a second, and I'll phone for you. Just take a seat."

Katya walked to a sunny spot where they could view the courtyard below and took a seat, motioning for Ace to sit opposite her. "Okay. They know you here." She thought a moment. "That woman—the hospital is named for her. She's your mother?"

"Was. She died, as I said, when I was young." Ace sank into the grey cushioned chair and rubbed his face.

Katya shook her head. "But they do know—that nurse knows who you are." She leaned forward and pulled his hands from his face, clasping them.

"She knows I'm a frequent visitor, that I spend a lot of time with the hospital's board members and that I take a tour now and then of the place when I'm here. What she doesn't know is that I am *Alexei Ivanovich* Elliott, one of two founders of this hospital."

"I thought..."

"Alexei Carter Ivanovich Elliott, named Alexei for my mother's father, Carter for my father's best friend, and Elliott for my own father, since I share his last name." He seemed to study her reaction and seemed satisfied when she blinked and leaned forward. "Ever watch kindergarten children trying to write their names? Ivanovich is a bitch when you're six years old. After Mom died, Dad had me shorten my name so it was easier to write in school."

"Therefore...Ace."

"Precisely." He rubbed her wrists with his thumbs then brought her hands to his lips and kissed her softly. "It's an open wound, so tread lightly, okay?"

Katya nodded. "Why all the secrecy?" She was openly curious, not caring at this point which one of them had an advantage. She wanted to know more about him.

"My father and my grandfather had a falling out when my mother died. I think *Ded Alexei* is the reason my father Americanised my name, too. In fact, I'm sure of it."

Old Alexei, of course. If Randal and Svetlana's father had disagreed on something, or if there had been hard feelings between them, Randal wouldn't wish a constant reminder that his son had been named for his father-in-law.

"Your grandparents are both alive, I hope?"

He nodded. "I call my *babooshka* Baba Jo—her name is Josephina. She and my grandfather live in Kansas City, and I visit them every time I am here. He is the second founder of the hospital, and she is the third. We wanted to keep everything in the family until we were in the black."

"This is what you've done with the monies from your game company," she guessed.

"Yes."

Katya lifted her arms and touched his face with both hands. "You never told your father? I'm sure he'd be very proud of you."

"My father thinks I'm irresponsible because I play video games as an adult. He isn't aware that I own my own company or that I'm worth millions."

She sat back in surprise. "Really? You don't think he reads the papers?"

"I doubt he'd care if he did know. He considers me more my mother's child than his, one of those gypsy Russians, you know?" Ace snorted. "My brothers are all dark-haired with dark eyes, but I'm the only one who reminds the old man of Russia."

"No." Katya's voice was firm. "You remind him of his wife, of the woman he loved and lost. That's probably what hurts him."

"Yeah? Well, I guess we all have our pain." Ace's troubled dark eyes held defiance, and Katya knew that somewhere inside the six-feet-something of adult male flesh and bone was a small child with unresolved closure on old issues.

"Mr. Elliott?" The female voice startled them both. Katya looked up to find Beverly standing a few feet away. "The lab is ready for you."

* * * *

Ace was glad Katya had stayed with him, despite his obvious moodiness. He would have willingly agreed to the test, to the inconvenience and discomfort of the bone marrow transplant—this was one of his children! What he resented was having everyone know his personal business, having them expect him to do the right thing when he'd have done it anyway.

He wanted to visit his son on his own, without everyone witnessing his first encounter with Nik. His heart broke for the child, having to endure the loneliness of staying in a hospital room while the rest of the family shared Thanksgiving dinner, while his friends played and relaxed on their brief vacation from school.

The weather was bitter cold. He'd forgotten what Midwestern winter weather was like, and the difference in temperatures from Australia, where it was summer, to blistering cold winds, ice and snow of Kansas City. Ace could feel the changes in his bones, even though he was inside a secure, well-insulated building.

Katya touched his arm as they left the lab. "We're expected for dinner. Do you mind?"

Ace shook his head. "I'd like to visit Nik later on my own, when everyone else is home, if that's okay."

She smiled, her eyes brimming with unshed tears. "I think he'd like that."

Ace frowned. "Why are you crying?"

Katya took a deep breath and sighed, her composure cracking. "I'm grateful to you. We all are."

There it was again, that doubt in her voice, like there would have been another choice for him. "He deserves everything we can do for him."

"Still. You didn't have to do this."

Indignation made him swell with anger, and he couldn't find an outlet for it other than to verbalise how he felt. "Yes, I did! I'm not some callous bastard who could turn his back on his own son!"

"I didn't mean to offend you!" She shrank from him. "I'm just trying to say thank you."

Ace was immediately sorry he'd snapped at her. He took her arm and led her towards the elevators. "Tell me about him. Does he even know who I am? Would he even want to meet me, or would it be better if I waited until he was asleep before visiting his room?"

She stepped into the compartment as the doors opened. "He knows. Elena told both kids after their parents died."

Great. Ace wondered what Elena had said to them? Did she go into details of how they'd never even been an itch in their father's pants, that he'd just wanted money for college? What the hell did adults say to kids who weren't planned?

Then it hit him. Sure, they were planned. *And wanted.* They were somebody's dream come true, and he'd helped provide the means. Maybe his father hadn't wanted him, but those children he'd fathered were definitely cherished.

He winced guiltily. He'd never felt unwanted. He was unsure what made him think otherwise.

Ace touched his own face with trembling hands once he'd pushed the button for their floor. Emotions he wasn't even aware of owning seemed to clench like a fist around his heart.

Katya leaned against him, pulled his hands away, and kissed his cheek. "I think you're brave for doing this."

He snorted. "For what? Taking a blood test?"

"You know what I mean."

He gazed into her eyes and wanted to kiss her. For all he knew, Katya was the one person in the world who empathised with him. She was certainly the only person he'd confided in regarding his mother.

When he was able to speak, he cleared his throat. "I'd like to go to the hotel and check in before we head over to your parents' place. Guess I need to call Dave and have him meet us at his car so we can retrieve our luggage."

Katya nodded, and Ace knew that she would go with him, that even if she didn't fully understand what he was feeling, she was aware that he wanted her with him.

* * * *

Katya hoped Ace didn't see her accompanying him as some sort of self-sacrifice on her part. She didn't want him to be alone. Maybe he was used to doing things on his own, not relying on anyone else, but her instincts warned her that this was different from any experience he'd had prior. He was vulnerable, even if he didn't realise it.

Dave insisted on driving them to the hotel, and the entire trip, which lasted all of fifteen minutes, Katya and Ace sat behind her sister and his brother, clasping hands.

This is a good man. Katya glanced at Ace's impenetrable expression. His eyes were dark, mysterious, glittering like black gold. His lips formed a grim line, and she longed to kiss him, to soften his expression.

Within minutes, they'd said goodbye to Dave and Elena, and she'd stood beside Ace as he went through the procedures of checking into his room. A strange fluttering in her stomach made her long to stand beside him, to link her arm through his, to reassure him that it was okay for him to feel whatever it was he was feeling. This was no business venture — it was a journey of self-discovery, and she doubted Ace had a clue as to how kind, decent, and caring he was.

Another elevator ride. Katya once again leaned against panelled walls, watching Ace punch buttons. She wondered just how many elevators Ace had used during the past few years. Where did Ace call home? Did he have a bedroom with personal belongings, an apartment or house with photographs, items he'd collected during his travels?

By the time he'd placed the key card in the receptacle on their door, Katya was ready to do whatever was required to push past Ace's defences and reach that untouchable region of his heart he'd protected over the years. He seemed shocked when she pushed him onto the bed and began undressing him.

"Katya?" He tried to capture her hands in his, but she pushed him away.

"Not this time, Ace. It's my turn to seduce you, and I'll do it if it takes all night."

"Katya, you don't have to do this."

She unbuckled his belt and unzipped his pants, keeping eye contact with him the entire time. "Do I look like someone has a gun to my head, forcing me?" She swatted his ass as she yanked on his pants to pull them off his hips. She boldly but gently grasped his balls and cock, smiling. "You telling me that you don't want me, that you feel pressured to perform?"

He rolled her onto her back, glaring at her. "What are you playing at? You think I need some kind of reward for doing right by Nik?"

"This has nothing to do with Nik."

"Yeah?" His voice was deep and breathy. "Then why?"

Katya locked her legs around his hips and rolled him onto his back as easily as he'd flipped her body moments earlier. "I want you." She rubbed her pussy against his crotch, took his hands in hers and guided him to her slit. "Wet, Ace. Warm, wet, and ready for you—just you. This isn't some form of misguided gratitude. It's sex, pure and simple. My body cuddling yours, your body inside mine and I'm not accepting no as your response."

"I don't get it."

She smiled. "Let's just say that the next time you help make a baby, you'll do it the old-fashioned way if I have any say in the matter." She grasped his wrists and pushed them above his head as he started to protest. "Ace, I'm not asking you for a baby—I'm asking you to relax, to fuck me, to give us both the goddamned time of day."

The perplexed look on his face gave her the giggles. "When's the last time you let yourself go, really gave yourself one-hundred percent to something other than your work?" She thrilled to the stiff cock rising beneath her ass. "I don't want anything from you other than the chance to know you better." She felt herself blush. "Okay, that and I want to fuck you again. There's no storm outside, only the one inside this room, and…don't make me beg."

He finally seemed to take the hint. The next thing she knew, his hands were on her body, as if memorising her form.

Ace couldn't remember the last time a woman other than Katya had seduced him. *What is wrong with you?* His mind splintered into a million thoughts that refused to cohere. *She's beautiful, intelligent, giving.* Ace switched midstream to thoughts of himself. *You're selfish, stubborn, afraid to commit…*

Once his thoughts became personal, he found he was chastising himself, giving her the benefit of better traits. *Wait a damn minute.* He looked inwardly once more. *I'm a helluva guy. Honest, dependable, and, oh, God, I'm horny right now.*

"What is it about you?" He was startled to find he'd voiced his thoughts this time.

Katya's breath seemed to catch in her throat. "I don't understand."

Ace kissed her lips tenderly. "I find myself wanting to please you for the hell of it. I picked up something for you at the airport in Sydney then again in Hilo, and I don't know why I haven't given you the presents. Well, I was pissed off on Hilo." He grinned sheepishly. "After that, I guess I didn't want you to consider them a bribe of some sort."

He rolled onto his back and laughed. "Which is ridiculous, considering you're the one with the best motive for bribing *me.*"

Katya gasped. "I am not bribing you!" She rose to a sitting position. "Is that what you think, that I'm having sex with you to get you to help Nik?"

Ace heard the hurt in her voice. "No." He looped an arm about her waist and pulled her alongside him again. "I've already had the blood test, which is pretty indicative that I'll go along with the surgery if I'm a match."

"Then why all the political assumptions?" She looked up at him imploringly. "Why are you analysing my reason for being here tonight?"

"Because it's what I do?" He laughed again. "Shit, I question everything and everyone, so don't feel special just because I'm singling you out."

"Yeah?" She rose again, this time to her knees and straddled him. "Analyse this, smart guy."

Next thing Ace knew, she was crouching, lowering herself so that her mouth was aligned with his cock, which he feared would explode before she so much as touched her lips to it.

The inside of her mouth felt so good, her tongue like warm velvet as it rasped and swirled around his shaft and balls. With every subtle flick and suckle, he felt himself sliding deeper and deeper into a vortex of physical comfort and emotional agony.

"Katya!" His body went rigid with want, and his hands sought her hair and shoulders. If only he could hold her closer while she did this, if only his mind could clench hers as she possessed him body and soul.

Her hands slid beneath him to grasp his hips and pull him deeper inside her mouth. Ace felt like he was home. *Home.* For the first time in years, he felt comforted, wanted, needed and truly cherished.

He couldn't concentrate—random thoughts slammed and rebounded. His pulse raced, and he felt a sudden mingling of relinquishing control with capturing something that had eluded him.

Katya was insistent, not coaxing him anymore but demanding...demanding what, though? Ace struggled to keep from coming, fought to regain control of his shattering senses. He should be doing this to her—he should be the one eliciting such a response from his partner.

Ace's fingers swept through her hair on his stomach. Her blonde, silken mane weakened his resolve, disavowing his reluctance to master his senses.

All of a sudden, he realised what he'd been missing in his life. A sweet surrender tugged at his heart as his cock swelled. A feeling of absolute calm swept over him in tandem with a rage to...give.

He groaned, voicing both his desire to give to her and his delirious demand for more attention. "Please, Katya—I want to feel myself inside of you. Ride me, baby, please—let me feel your pussy on my cock."

When she lifted her head and slid upwards, Ace grasped her around the waist and helped position her. The ache for her was so strong he could barely contain himself.

Katya tossed her hair, baring her throat and breasts, and Ace leaned forward hungrily, kissing first one breast and then the other, his hands and mouth greedily seeking the taste and touch of what drove him mad with need.

A little longer, please. He wasn't sure who he begged, himself or a higher power. All he knew was that he had to prolong the pain.

Katya, however, apparently refused to be denied. She reached beneath her and cupped his balls, stroking gently, urging him with her voice as well as her hands. "Come for me, Ace, please, come for me."

Dusha. Ace thought of the Russian word for dear or darling. *That's what she is to me*, he thought in surprise. If her goal had been to insinuate herself into his heart, mission accomplished.

He stopped resisting and gave her what she wanted, his full attention, his seed, his adoration. He pulled her face to his and kissed her with a passion he'd never known, wrapping her in his arms and holding her as close as possible as he came. Everything hit him at once, his children, his father and brothers, the woman in his arms. Knowing he'd soon be meeting her family. His emotions read like a Chinese menu, taking a bit of angst from column A, adding to the joy in column B, tossed together with every apprehension imaginable in column C, and sprinkled liberally with the "Oh, shit, what next?" factor.

Katya didn't keep him waiting for what came next. As they cuddled after sex, she nibbled on his earlobe. "Ace?"

"Yes?"

"I'm hungry."

* * * *

Smells evoked powerful memories, as did sounds and it had been a long time since he'd paid attention to his senses. Now, Ace inhaled deeply, taking in the aromas of candles on the mantle at Katya's parents' home and the pinecones in a bucket near the hearth. It pained him to think that he couldn't remember how his mother's house had smelled, but he could well imagine her here, chatting with the women, hugging Nina, exchanging looks with her beloved.

When Katya looked up to find him staring at her, a longing tugged at Ace's heart, a desire to be with her, not just in body but in spirit. He heard, for the first time, not just the laughter in the room, but the silences, the shared looks that spoke volumes between mothers and daughters and the intonation of love without words between Dave and Elena.

Is this how love sounds? He listened to his heart. Quiet, peaceful, rhythmic silence washed over him. Katya held out her hand, and he knew without crossing to her what she'd feel like, that her flesh in his would be soft, warm, inviting.

Ace's peripheral vision gathered the information the room offered, the people and the sounds they made, the things that they wore or had collected, but his tunnel vision narrowed so that all he really saw was Katya. It was too soon to tell, but he suspected that some day she would fill his life completely, that his glimpse of her here was only a precursor to seeing her occupying much more than one slice of life for him.

He hugged Katya then spied Randal. "I'd like to meet my son now." Ace stepped back from her and walked towards his father. Once awkward hugs were exchanged, he took a deep breath. "Want to join me, meet your grandson?"

Randal's eyes filled with tears. "I've already met him, son, but I'll go with you."

Ace's voice choked with emotion as he tried to joke with his father. "You're not ashamed to be seen with me?"

"Just no stopping off at the sperm bank on the way there." Randal winked then chuckled.

Before Ace could recover from the shock that his dad had dared joke about such a thing, Katya slid her arm through his. "Trust me, Mr. Elliott, those days are behind him. He'll be too busy to even contemplate such a thing."

While everyone else laughed nervously, Baba Lidia made a sour face. "You two come back here tomorrow. I teach you how to cook." She held out her hands, palms up. "What? You gotta know how to do more than *that* if you're to make a life."

Make a life. Ace felt happier than he'd ever felt, because that was exactly what he intended to learn how to do.

About the Authors

Summer Devon

Summer Devon is the alter ego Kate Rothwell who invented Summer's name in the middle of a nasty blizzard whilst talking to her sister who longed to visit some friends in Devon, England, so the name Summer Devon is all about desire. Kate/Summer lives in Connecticut, USA and also writes gaslight historicals under her own name.

Summer has a blog and a MySpace page, so be sure to catch up with her at Summer's Blog and at her myspace page.

Summer is also involved with a couple of groups but the one she's been a part of the longest is Romance Unleashed. So, be sure to catch up with me at any of these places.

Alexis Fleming

Alexis Fleming is one of those strange people who live inside their mind. No, she doesn't hear little voices... Well, she does, just not the type you're thinking of.

Alexis's world is peopled with interesting characters and exciting possibilities that come to life in each and every book she writes. Her first love has always been romance, whether on this world or the next. Hot, sizzling relationships with a dash of comedy and a few trials and tribulations thrown in to test her characters.

When she's not tied to her computer creating sizzling stories to tempt her readers, she helps run a busy motel set on the edge of a National Marine Park in Australia. What better place to get inspiration for the tales she turns out? A glorious sunset over the ocean, dolphins playing almost in her front yard, suntanned bodies lazing on the sand... How could she not get caught up in the eroticism of that?

Lyn Cash

Lyn Cash is the multi-published author of over fifty short stories and confessions, a couple of non-fiction books, and over a dozen novellas and novels. Her mainstream fiction is written under Bobbie Cole and her erotic fiction under the pen names of Lyn Cash and Cash Cole.

Total-e-Bound Publishing

www.total-e-bound.com

Take a look at our exciting range of literagasmic™
erotic romance titles and discover pure quality
at Total-E-Bound.

www.ingramcontent.com/pod-product-compliance
Lightning Source LLC
Chambersburg PA
CBHW020432180626
46812CB00003B/1200